"Ugh!" PJ  ie lunchroom. "Do you smell that

I sure did. It was one of the grossest things that's ever gone in or out of my nostrils, if you get my drift.

"It's worse than that dead squirrel in our chimney!" Keisha said, holding her nose.

"Where the heck is it coming from?" Fernando asked.

"I think it's in there!" I said, pointing to the kitchen door. Then suddenly, a loud whirring sound, like from a blender or some kind of machine, came from behind the door.

"Someone's in there!" Keisha said.

"Maybe it's them! Let's go in!" said PJ.

We walked slowly up to the kitchen door—we kind of had to get used to the smell bit by bit. Finally, we knocked. "Brian? You in there?" I yelled. No answer. The machine noise had to be drowning me out anyway. I signaled to the rest of the Crew to follow me, and swung the door open.

⟫◆⟪

**Other Books in
The Kinetic City
Super Crew Series**

This School Stinks!

The Case of the Secret Scent

J. A. Warner

**LEARNING
TRIANGLE
P R E S S**

*Connecting
kids, parents, and teachers
through learning*

An imprint of McGraw-Hill

New York   San Francisco   Washington, D.C.   Auckland   Bogotá   Caracas
Lisbon   London   Madrid   Mexico City   Milan   Montreal   New Delhi
San Juan   Singapore   Sydney   Tokyo   Toronto

McGraw-Hill

A Division of The McGraw·Hill Companies

Library of Congress Cataloging-in-Publication Data applied for.

1 2 3 4 5 6 7 8 9 0 DOC/DOC 9 0 3 2 1 0 9 8

ISBN 0-07-006695-7

The sponsoring editor for this book was Judith Terrill-Breuer, the senior producer was Joe Shepherd, the editing supervisor was Maureen B. Walker, and the production supervisor was Clare B. Stanley. It was set in Century Old Style by Dennis J. Smith of McGraw-Hill's Professional Book Group in Hightstown, New Jersey.

Printed and bound by R.R. Donnelley & Sons Company.

McGraw-Hill books are available at special quantity discounts to use as premiums and sales promotions. For more information, please write to the Director of Special Sales, McGraw-Hill, 11 West 19th Street, New York, NY 10011. Or contact your local bookstore.

Contents

About the Crew

It is the near future. Peace has broken out all over the world, and the President of the United States has decided to donate the world's most sophisticated military vehicle, the X-100 Advanced Tactical Vehicle, to "the youth of America, that they might use this powerful tool to learn, to explore, and to help others."

Since the X-100 was designed in a top-secret factory in Kinetic City, the vehicle was renamed **The Kinetic City Express** and the first young crew was dubbed the **Kinetic City Super Crew**.

But who would be the members of the Crew? Kinetic City's mayor, Richard M. Schwindle, puts out a call to the young people of the city. Many answer the call, and seven are chosen: Keisha, Derek, Megan, Curtis, Fernando, PJ, and Max.

Now the Crew travel the world, along with their talkative supercomputer, ALEC, in a tireless quest for truth, justice, and the perfect deep-dish pizza. Their quest may never end.

About the Train

CIA Top Secret Document #113057
DECLASSIFIED: 9/12/99

Originally designed to carry military intelligence teams to trouble spots throughout the world, the X-100 is capable of ultra-high-speed travel, under the control of the Advanced Logic Electronic Computer (ALEC) Series 9000. The vehicle can travel over land on existing train tracks and on tank-style treads. For crossing bodies of water, the X-100 can seal its waterproof bulkheads and travel underwater, using an advanced form of Magneto-Hydrodynamic Drive propulsion. The X-100 has several small vehicles within it which can travel with or without human passengers, including a small submarine and a jet copter. Finally, the X-100 has sophisticated information-gathering capabilities, using 'round-the-clock, high-speed access to the Internet, an extensive CD-ROM library, and the ability to generate realistic science simulations in its "Cyber Car."

THE PHONE CALL

"Kinetic City Super Crew! When you want the facts, we hit the tracks! Curtis speaking!"

"Hey, Curtis, it's Brian! Something stinks at my new school!"

"Yeah, I know. The football team, right?"

"No, I mean something *really* stinks! You've got to check it out! The smell is killing us!"

CHAPTER ONE

Something Rotten in Peak Valley

Kinetic City Express Journal: "This School Stinks: The Case of the Secret Scent." Curtis reporting. It all started one crisp fall morning, when Brian Kim called the KC Hotline. Brian was my lab partner in science class last year. We used to rag on each other all the time. It wasn't mean—more like a sport. He'd bug me about not being up on the latest bands and clothes, and I'd get on his case about nearly setting the school on fire every time he used any of the lab equipment. But underneath all of that, we pretty much got along.

I hadn't heard from Brian since his family moved from Kinetic City to Peak

Valley, just a few miles away. He had transferred to Peak Valley High, and I figured he needed some time to get to know people over there. Especially since Brian's the kind of guy who has to know everybody. I sure didn't know anyone else who'd have lunch with the chess club one day and the football team the next without missing a beat. No matter who you were, he'd always find something to talk about.

Anyway, Brian told me everything had been fine at Peak Valley High so far, until Monday afternoon's debate team practice. (Brian's a natural at debating. I think it's partly because he knows a lot and partly because he just likes to argue.) The team was getting ready for a big match against Snurdburg High in two weeks. Then, all of a sudden, the whole room started to stink! He said it smelled kind of like rotten eggs, or maybe an oil refinery. It smelled so rank that they couldn't even finish practicing.

4

That was weird, but Brian hoped it was a one-time thing. No such luck. The next day, he and his new band, Bucket, were rehearsing for the Homecoming party in the school's music room. About twenty minutes into the set, the smell came back! It was the same smell that knocked out the debate team, and it was as raunchy as ever. That's when Brian decided it was time to call in the Super Crew.

After I got off the phone with Brian, I took a quick walk through the KC Express train and rounded up the other Crew members. I found Fernando in the Lounge Car watching his favorite '50s monster movie, <u>It Came from the Back of the Refrigerator</u>. PJ was in the Gym Car shooting baskets. The three of us met up with Keisha in the Control Car. That's the train's high-tech command center, where we have all our important meetings. When we walked in, we were greeted with a smile and a really weird smell . . .

"Hey, Crew!" Keisha said cheerfully. "I just whipped up some hot chocolate in the Kitchen Car! Want some?"

She handed me the first cup, since I was closest. In fact, I think I caught Fernando and PJ backing away. The smell got stronger. It reminded me of DiNuzio's Pizza. Normally, that's good—but coming out of hot chocolate, it was pretty gross.

"Um, thanks, Keisha," I said. I took a little sip just to be polite. That was a mistake. It tasted even worse than it smelled.

Keisha obviously noticed I wasn't loving it. "What's the matter?" she asked, tugging nervously at her track-team sweatshirt. "Not enough sugar?"

I shrugged. She stopped to blow her nose, and then reached over and grabbed a canister she'd brought in with her. It was full of something that *looked* like sugar—except maybe a little too yellow. "I never put enough in to start," she said, handing it to me. "Go ahead and put more in if you want."

"Wait a second," Fernando said. He took the canister from me, stuck his nose in it, and sniffed. "Whoa!" he said, jerking his head back. "This isn't sugar! It's *garlic powder!*"

That explained why I was thinking of DiNuzio's pizza. They put a lot of garlic on it, and they always have big shakers of garlic powder on the table.

"Uh-oh!" Keisha said. She took the canister from Fernando and sniffed hard. Her nostrils made a loud SNNNNORRRFF! sound. Then she looked a little embarrassed.

"Sorry," she said. "I've got a stuffy nose from my allergies. I can barely smell this at all. It looked like sugar, so I just dumped it in." She looked up at me and started giggling. "You should have seen the look on your face!" she said. She twisted her face into this really goofy pucker, and then burst out laughing. Fernando and PJ laughed with her. It's nice when you can entertain people, isn't it?

Once things settled down, I looked at them and said, "So, does anyone want to hear about the case?"

"Sure," Fernando replied with a smirk. "May as well, as long as we're here." It was a typical 'Nando comment. He doesn't take himself, or being on the Crew, too seriously. Sometimes it's a little annoying, but it can be refreshing, too.

"Okay," I said. "To make a long story short, my friend Brian says there's some awful smell around Peak Valley High."

"Hold on," Fernando said. He pushed his colorful knit cap back to reveal a scruffy mop of wavy dark hair. "We're going to spend this whole case wandering around a school that reeks?"

It was the perfect cue to introduce my contribution to the mission. "Exactly what I thought, Fernando," I said. "That's why we're all bringing these." I reached under the main control panel and pulled out our first line of defense: a box of military-issue, ultra-filtered, super-lightweight high-tech gas masks. There were plenty to go around. I stuck one on my head to model it. The Crew didn't seem impressed.

"What? What's the matter?" I asked.

"You look like a dork," PJ replied. She doesn't mince words. Sometimes I wish she did. Even though she's two years younger than I and nearly a foot shorter, she could really make me feel small.

"Where'd you get that thing?" Keisha asked. At least she was trying to keep a straight face.

"In the old supply room," I explained. "Must have been left over from when the KC Express was a military train. Sure, they look a little funny, but this way, we'll be protected from whatever's stinking up the place."

"Chill out, Curtis," Keisha said. "This isn't a chemical weapons plant. This is just a bad smell at some high school. We can handle it."

"What makes you so sure this smell is so harmless?" I asked. Now I had their attention.

Sure, my Crew mates can act tough and cool, but sometimes, it's just because they haven't considered the danger of a situation. Not me. I think of *every* possible danger.

"Think of it," I said. "Smells are gases. Some gases are poisonous. *Now* do you want to walk in there unarmed?"

"Oh, I don't know, Curtis. I really don't think it's going to be a big deal," Keisha said.

"Yeah, besides, if the gas was poisonous, wouldn't Brian be in the hospital right now?" PJ asked.

"I don't know," I said. "Maybe it's slow-acting poison."

The others didn't look convinced, but they also looked like they didn't want to argue anymore. "Fine, bring the masks," Fernando said. "Just take that one off for now, will you? I can't talk to you seriously while you're wearing that thing."

I pulled my mask off and put it in the box. Sometimes I think the Crew doesn't appreciate the way I think ahead. I like to think that with the right gadget, you can be prepared for everything. Sometimes I'll find that gadget, like I did with these masks, but a lot of time I'll just invent one myself with my high-tech know-how. That's why they call me Curtis the Can-Man. Sure, my inventions don't always work perfectly the first time, but hey—that's all part of the game.

"Well, let's see if we can figure out what this smell is," Keisha said, whipping out her notebook. "Give me the facts, Curtis. What did Brian say it smelled like?"

"Rotten eggs," I replied.

"Well, this case is open and shut," Fernando said. "It must be fancy bean week at the cafeteria. That'll get the whole student body tooting like a ska band's horn section."

"Tooting, as in . . . ?" I asked, trying to keep things businesslike.

"Passing gas. Breaking wind. Honking. Firing up the rear engines. Talking out the wrong side."

"Are you through?" Keisha asked, cutting him off.

"I'm just getting started," Fernando replied, as a sly grin broke out across his narrow face. "I've got a million of 'em . . ."

"Let's save the rest for later, then," PJ said, stopping him before he went on. "Curtis, what do you think of Fernando's . . . um, 'tooting' theory?"

"Well, I guess we can't rule it out," I said. "But if the gas were coming from something like that, you'd think Brian would have figured it out himself."

"Maybe something died in one of the air vents," Keisha offered. "Like a bird or a squirrel. That happened in our fireplace flue once. It was nasty. Until we figured it out, you couldn't even go near our living room. It kind of smelled a little like rotten eggs."

"Good idea," I said. "Although I'm not sure it fits what's going on. The smell's popped up in two completely different parts of the school."

"How about the easy answer?" PJ asked. "Could there be rotten eggs in those rooms? Like, in somebody's lunch?"

"I don't think so," I said. "This stuff was all going on after school. Nobody had any lunch with them."

"Why don't we see what ALEC's got to say?" Fernando suggested. "Maybe he can tell us what else smells like rotten eggs."

"Sure thing," I replied. I began tapping on the keys of our supercomputer's massive command console. "I'll fire him up now."

Before I go on, I guess I should tell you a few things about ALEC. He's one of the world's most powerful supercomputers and definitely the coolest. His monitor takes up an entire wall of the Control Car, and his memory banks are full of information about everything from aardvarks to zephyrs. He was built especially for the KC Express train by Dr. Alexander Graham Cracker, a super-genius scientist who lives alone deep in an uncharted rain forest.

I call ALEC "he" and not "it" for two reasons. One is that his artificial intelligence is so sophisticated that sometimes, he seems almost human. In fact, that can be one of his drawbacks. There have been more than a few times when he gave us some information we didn't really need, and when we told him, he seemed disappointed—maybe even a little hurt. Like once, he spent all day downloading an amazing virtual fingerpaint game. Too bad what we asked him about were finger*prints*. When we broke the news to him, he was so embarrassed that he shut himself down for two days, like a kid locking himself in his room.

The other reason I think of ALEC as "alive" is that I'm pretty much in charge of him. Sure, everyone in the Crew uses ALEC on cases. But when ALEC himself goes a little haywire, I'm the one who usually steps in to fix him up. That's because I'm the nuts-and-bolts guy on the Super Crew. I've always known computers inside and out—and believe me, whatever I didn't know before working on ALEC, I know

now. And spending all that time keeping ALEC running smoothly (and listening to him chit-chat while I fix his circuits) has made me a little attached to him, in spite of all his quirks.

One of those quirks is spouting out really strange factoids every time we fire him up. Today was no exception. "Helllloooo, Crew!" ALEC yelped happily as his monitor snapped on. "Did you know that three and a half billion years ago, tiny one-celled bacteria evolved the ability to swim toward food and away from poison? That's a behavior called chemotaxis!"

See what I mean? "That's great, ALEC," I told him, the way I used to praise my little brother when he blew his nose by himself. "But we need to talk about a strange smell."

"Well, then, I'm already on the right track!" ALEC chirped with delight. "Chemotaxis is considered to be a primitive form of smell— and perhaps the first sense ever to evolve in living organisms! Both chemotaxis and smelling are ways of sensing chemicals in the environment."

"So our noses are basically chemical detectors?" I asked, getting a little sidetracked myself.

"Huh. I never thought of it that way," PJ added.

"Well, it's true!" ALEC replied. "Every distinctive odor—from chocolate chip cookies to skunk spray—is basically a unique combination of chemicals in the air. Those chemicals waft up your nostrils, and lock onto nerve cells deep in your upper nose. Then those signals send impulses straight to your brain, which helps you identify the smell!"

"Well, we just got a call about a smell that nobody can identify," Keisha said, getting down to the facts. "It's over at Peak Valley High School."

"This guy doesn't know where it's coming from, but he says it smells like rotten eggs," I explained. "You know anything that smells like that?"

DING! ALEC's monitor lit up instantly. "Yes: Rotten eggs!" he announced happily.

That was his real answer. Like I said before, sometimes computers just don't "get it."

"Besides that, ALEC," PJ said impatiently.

"Oh," ALEC replied, sounding just a little hurt. "I didn't realize you'd already thought of that. Let me check my database . . . I've got eczema, Edam cheese, Edward V, eggs . . . eggs comma fried, eggs comma poached, ah ha! Eggs comma rotten. Smells of."

"What's it say?" Keisha asked.

"The smell of rotten eggs is caused by bacteria that produce sulfur-based chemicals as they digest the egg material," ALEC recited from his database.

"Okay, so it's this sulfur stuff that smells, then," Fernando said. "Where else does sulfur come from?"

ALEC began a series of PINGS as he rattled off the names. "Let's see . . . sulfur comes from paper mills, oil refinery emissions, people . . ."

"Hold on, ALEC," I said. "People?"

"That's right, Curtis," he replied. "The bacteria that live in the human digestive system often produce smelly sulfur gases. That's the distinctive odor in human flatulence."

"Flatulence?" PJ asked.

"You know . . . blowing a backwards raspberry," Fernando said.

"Oh," she said. She tried to look professional, but I caught her stifling a giggle.

"We've been over that, ALEC," Keisha jumped in. "Got anything else?"

ALEC's hard drive whirred for a moment in deep thought. "Well, it's not a natural source, but gas companies do add sulfur compounds called mercaptans to natural gas."

"You mean they make it stink on purpose?" Fernando asked. "Why would anyone do that?"

"Because natural gas is odorless," ALEC replied. "And it's incredibly flammable. If it weren't, you wouldn't be able to heat a house or cook with it. So if the gas leaks, it can be very dangerous. One lit match and a whole house could explode!"

"Cool!" Fernando replied. I think he's seen too many movies. He's starting to confuse real life with entertainment.

"I think I get it," Keisha said, much more thoughtfully. "If they put the mercaptans in the gas, then people can smell a gas leak and get out in time."

"That's right!" ALEC replied with a big *bleep*. "And mercaptans are a good choice, since you humans are especially sensitive to them."

"Uh-oh," I said.

"Uh-oh what?" PJ asked.

"Don't you get it?" I said. My voice was getting louder, almost without me knowing it. "If Brian's smelling sulfur all over the school, the place could be springing gas leaks left and right!"

"Oh no!" Keisha said. "We'd better call over there and make sure they check it out. If there really is a gas leak, the whole school could blow up!"

"ALEC, auto-dial Peak Valley High School for us!" PJ said.

"Right away, Crew!" ALEC replied. "I'll put on the speakerphone!"

The KC Hotline's speakerphone flipped on. We heard seven lightning-fast beeps and then a few rings from the other end of the phone line. Then an answering machine picked up with a *click*. An extremely calm male voice was on the recorded message.

"Hello. You've reached Peak Valley Higher Learning Center. This is Principal Marsh. No one can take your call right now. Why not drop by and say hello instead? We all could use a hug." With that, there was another click and a dial tone. They didn't even give us a chance to leave a message.

"Well, *that* was weird," I said.

"Sounds like we'd better take the principal up on his offer," Keisha said.

"You mean we're going to get a hug?" Fernando said with a laugh.

"Not *that* offer, smart guy," she said, shaking her head. Keisha likes to joke around too—in fact, she has a weakness for bad puns—but Fernando could be a little much for her sometimes. "I mean we'd better go over there in person before the whole school blows up!"

"You said it, Keisha!" PJ chimed in. "ALEC! Set course for Peak Valley High School!"

"Right away, Crew!" ALEC replied. His circuits sprang to life and turbo-charged the train with a burst of energy.

We were off. It would only take a few minutes to get to Peak Valley. I just hoped we'd get there in time.

CHAPTER TWO

Class Dismissed!

We rode the KC Express up as close to Peak Valley as we could—but still far enough away that flying bits of blown-up school wouldn't damage it. As we stepped out of the train and got our first glimpse of the school, I was relieved to see that it <u>didn't</u> have a big hole blown out of it. Unfortunately, we couldn't be sure it would stay that way. We ran up to the front entrance, hoping we wouldn't be caught there at just the wrong time.

We figured we'd have to go through some kind of security system, but we ended up just walking right through the main doors into a deserted hallway. I was pretty surprised. Even at Kinetic City High School, which isn't exactly Fort Knox, you can't just walk in there if you're not a student. Someone would stop you and ask who you were. Here, it looked like we were on our own.

So the first thing we did was stop and smell the air. It smelled, all right. But it smelled like a lot of different things . . .

"I don't know about rotten eggs, but I think I smell vanilla somewhere," PJ said.

"I think I smell lavender, actually," Keisha said. "My mom has some soap that smells like that." The air did smell kind of nice, for a place that was supposed to stink.

Fernando was already sniffing around further down the hall. "It's different down here," he said, waving us over. "I think I got a whiff of that rotten egg stuff."

I jogged over to where he was. It was faint, but I could smell it. Now that I smelled it, it kind of reminded me of the gas stove over at my cousin's house. "That's it," I called to the others. "Smells like gas."

24

"Then we've got to clear this place out—and fast," Keisha called back. She walked up to a door near the main entrance. "Hey, here's the principal's office. Come on, let's see if he's in."

Fernando and I ran over to join the others. We knocked, waited a second, and then went in. The lights were off, but the whole room glowed from the light of what looked like about a million candles. That lavender soap smell Keisha was talking about got a lot stronger. PJ flipped on the overhead light.

It was the weirdest principal's office I've ever seen. Everything was in these soft pink and pale green colors—it almost looked like a baby's room. There were big chunks of purple and blue crystal sitting on the desk and bookshelves, along with all the candles. *Lit* candles. Uh-oh. *Fire + Gas Leak = Kingdom Come,* I thought to myself.

"Hey, Crew!" I yelled nervously. "We've got some open flames in here!"

I started blowing them out, but there were dozens of them. And some were up way too high, so I couldn't reach them. I only got through five or six candles when all of a sudden I heard PJ's voice behind me.

"Stand back, Curtis!" she commanded. I turned around. She had a big tank slung over her shoulder, and a nozzle pointed at me. She looked like some kind of futuristic space trooper. Then I realized what her weapon was and jumped out of the way just before she opened fire.

WHOOOOOSH! In seconds, the whole room was covered in white, sticky foam. Including me. You never realize how messy a fire extinguisher can be until you actually use one.

"You could have given me another second to get out of the way," I said, wiping the foam off my shirt.

"No time for that, Curtis! One wasted second and this whole place could be blown to smithereens!" she said. I had to hand it to her—the candles *were* all out. I didn't want to be around when the principal got back, though.

Just then, Fernando spotted something. "Hey, look back there!" he said, pointing to a microphone in the back of the room. "That must be the mike for the PA system. Why don't we just make an announcement and evacuate the school ourselves?"

"I don't know," said Keisha. "Are we allowed to do that?"

"Who cares?" he replied, climbing over the principal's desk. "We've got a crisis situation here. Let's move!"

Fernando found a control panel next to the microphone, and started fiddling around with the dials and switches. All of a sudden, an eardrum-piercing, high-pitched squeal of feedback echoed through the halls. Ever hear fingernails scratch down a chalkboard? Try cranking it up to 10 on a guitar amplifier, and you'll have some idea of what this was like.

After recovering from the shock, Fernando turned a couple of the dials way back, and the noise went away. We all sighed with relief.

"Well, now that you've got their attention, why don't you do the talking?" PJ asked.

"Okay," Fernando said. He put his lips to the mike and tried out his best radio-DJ voice. "Um, good morning, everyone," he began. His voice reverberated out in the hallway behind us. "This is Fernando from the Kinetic City Super Crew. I have an important announcement to make, but we must ask that you do not panic."

For a second there was dead silence. He seemed to be handling it pretty well. He looked at us, and we nodded in support. Then he went on, keeping his voice calm and even.

"We have reason to believe there is a gas leak in the building, and we need everyone to evacuate immediately. Please don't run or push, but leave as quickly as possible, because the building may explode at any moment." He looked like he was finished, but then leaned back in. "That's all," he added, not knowing what else to say.

We stepped back outside the door and

into the hallway. There was a spooky silence in the air.

"Well, I guess we did all we could," I said.

"Yep," Keisha agreed. "It sure is quiet, though."

"Well, I told them not to panic," Fernando said. "See? When Nando talks, people listen."

Just then we heard a low rumbling from the stairwells and the other end of the hall. It grew louder and louder very fast. The rumble turned into the sound of hundreds and hundreds of rapid footsteps, underneath hundreds and hundreds of voices. We looked back at Fernando. He grinned sheepishly.

"Well, I also told them to move fast," he said. "See? When Nando talks . . ."

But we didn't hear anything else Fernando said. The stairway doors burst open, and a stampede of students and teachers rushed into the hall we were standing in. Within seconds, we were floating along in a river of running bodies, with no choice but to keep up with them. Meanwhile, another group was rounding the corner, and when they hit the hall the crowd became twice as thick.

I barely made it out the doors without being trampled. We all ran out—the Super Crew, the students, the teachers, and everyone else at Peak Valley High, emptying every corner of the school out onto the front lawn.

CHAPTER THREE

Off the Scent

It took only a few minutes for the entire school to evacuate. Luckily, everyone made it outside okay. Of course, now there were about a thousand teenagers, plus assorted teachers and staff members, standing on the lawn not knowing what to do with themselves. It was definitely time to look for someone in authority.

But the first person we ran into was Brian Kim. He wasn't standing with everyone else. Instead, he was hanging toward the back, looking just a little too cool to care about what was going on. His hair was a shade of purple today, and he was wearing baggy pants, an exotic vest, and what looked like a light bulb on a string around his neck . . .

"Hey, Curtis, over here!" Brian called over to me. I led my fellow Crew members over to meet him. I couldn't tell if Keisha looked interested or disgusted.

"How's it going?" I asked as we walked up to him. "Still blowing up the science labs?"

"They won't let me near anything dangerous yet," he laughed. "I've got a reputation." He gestured to the rest of the Crew. "I guess these are your partners?"

"Yep," I said. "This is PJ, Keisha, and Fernando."

"Whats," Brian said, shaking everyone's hand.

"What's what?" I asked.

"Just 'whats.' You know, instead of 'what's going on,' 'what's up,' you just say 'whats.' Right?" I had never heard of that. I just stared back at him.

"Sure, 'whats,'" Fernando said. "I've heard of that." I rolled my eyes at him. I'd never heard him say that in my life.

Brian was fooled, though. "See, your buddy

knows it," he said. "You gotta catch up to this decade sometime, Curtis," he said with a grin.

"This from a guy who wouldn't know a microchip from a chocolate chip," I shot back.

"Hey, I don't need to know how that electronic stuff works. That's why I've got guys like you to show me," he replied with a smirk. He wasn't kidding. When we wrote up our last lab report together he kept putting the floppy disks in the computer backwards. I had to pry them out with a screwdriver and some margarine. At least he made it up to me by picking me up some really cool Japanese game software at one of his secondhand stores.

By that time, PJ had been left out of the conversation for a while, so she decided to bring up what everyone was wondering about. "Hey Brian, what's with the light bulb around your neck?" she asked, pointing right at his Weird Clothing Accessory of the Week.

"Stands for power," Brian replied matter-of-factly. "Everyone in the underground trip-rap Austin cyber-salsa-funk scene wears 'em. If you're in the know. El Nino has over a hundred in his collection."

Keisha's eyes lit up. "You listen to El Nino? The Guatemalan electric trumpet player?"

"Yeah, you know him?" Brian asked. He sounded kind of surprised.

"Are you kidding? He rules!" Keisha said. "I never met anyone else who's heard of him before!"

"Well, I actually liked him better before he sold out," Brian said.

"Oh, right, yeah, I assumed that," Keisha replied. It sounded like they were having some kind of a contest or something. If they were, Brian may have finally met his match. Keisha has the biggest CD collection of anyone I've ever met. She likes almost every kind of music that's ever been invented, except maybe the stuff they used to make us sing at Spring Pageant in grade school.

"So, Brian, who do we talk to about this gas leak?" Fernando jumped in. "We should probably straighten this out."

"You want to find Marsh," he replied.

"Oh, you mean Principal Marsh?" Keisha asked. "The guy on the school voice mail?"

"We were just in his office," PJ said. "We didn't see him."

"Yeah, he kind of comes and goes," Brian explained. "He's still getting settled in. He just took over a few weeks ago, when Ms. Snidely left."

"He sure sounded . . . *interesting* on the phone," I said. I couldn't really come up with another word.

Brian understood what I meant, though. "Yeah, he's kind of a dork, but I'll take him over Snidely any day. That lady was sweet."

We all looked at each other. "I don't get it," PJ said. "If she was sweet, why didn't you like her?"

"Not sweet as in nice, sweet as in nasty and mean. You know what I'm talking about," Brian said. (Actually, we didn't.) "I'll tell you what, though, I wouldn't mind having to stand out here for a while. We were in the middle of this big state math exam that's going on all week. Getting let out of that was the worst."

"Wait—are you saying you *wanted* to stay in there and finish the exam?" I asked.

"Come on, Curtis, I mean the worst as in it was really good. You really do need to catch up on your street talk," Brian said. I guess maybe I did, if we were going to get any facts straight in this case. I've always thought Brian ought to come with his own dictionary.

Keisha was determined to get some information, though. "So, Brian, this nasty . . . er, I mean, *sweet* smell you were complaining about . . . could you smell it during the math exam?"

"Yeah. Not so much at first, but by the time you and the Super Posse showed up, it was stinking something awful in there."

"Awful as in . . . ?" Keisha asked.

"Awful as in really bad," Brian replied, looking a little confused. "That was really the first time the smell hit us in class. But it hit hard." He sniffed his shirt sleeve and made a face. "Ugh, I think it got in my clothes. Smell this," he said to me, sticking his sleeve right under my nose.

I tried not to inhale, but couldn't help catching a whiff. Rotten eggs again. It was worse on him than it had been in the hallway. "Whoa! That must be one serious gas leak," I said.

"Yeah, it's lucky we cleared out the school before anything happened," Keisha said.

"I just hope Principal Marsh won't get mad about what I did to his office," PJ said, looking a little embarrassed.

Brian laughed, and flipped back a purple lock of hair. "Trust me, Marsh doesn't get mad. That's him over there. Why don't you go drop jaw with him?"

I stopped and thought for just a second. "You mean talk?" I asked.

"You're catching on," Brian said with a wink. Then he waved to some friends and went over to "drop jaw" with them.

We walked over to the pudgy, apple-cheeked man Brian had pointed out. He was wearing big, round glasses, corduroy pants, and a fuzzy pastel sweater with a small bunny logo on the chest. He was walking in from the parking lot behind the school, looking very confused.

"Principal Marsh!" Keisha called to him as we approached.

"Oh, hello. You students must be new here. Otherwise you'd know that you can call me Leslie." He extended his hand.

"Actually, we don't go to school here," Fernando said. "We're the Kinetic City Super Crew. I'm Fernando, and this is Curtis, Keisha, and PJ." We all made our introductions.

"Oh, the Super Crew! I've heard so much about you. You kids sound like you have such positive energy," Principal Marsh . . . er, *Leslie*, said warmly. "Are you here to explain my students' little impromptu assembly? I just got back from a few errands and I have no idea what they're doing out here. I mean, I admire their spontaneity, but Outdoor Appreciation Hour isn't usually until one o'clock."

"As a matter of fact, Leslie, we brought everyone out here. We had to evacuate the school," I explained. "You've got a dangerous situation here."

"Oh no? What is it? Prickly nasties?" Leslie asked, looking worried. He rubbed his temples, as if a headache was coming on.

"Prickly nasties?" I asked.

"Yes! That's my little word for bad feelings and negative energy! If it's hit the school, it's all my fault! I didn't want to subject the kids to that math exam, but the state government made me!"

"Hold on, hold on," Keisha said. "We're not talking about the math exam. We're talking about a gas leak."

The principal blinked, then shook his head and chuckled. "A gas leak? Well, that can't be right! We don't use gas in this school. All our heating is electric . . . until we switch to windmill power, which I'm hoping to do by next fall. I'm building the plant out back in my spare time."

I didn't know whether to feel relieved or disappointed. I mean, it was great that there wasn't a gas leak, but it was also pretty embarrassing that we evacuated the whole school for nothing. I looked at my Crew mates and shrugged sheepishly.

Luckily, Fernando stepped in and kept things moving forward. "Well, that's good news," he said matter-of-factly. "But that also puts us back to square one in our investigation. We got a call about a strange smell at Peak Valley. Do you know anything about it, Principal Marsh?"

"You're not talking about my aromatherapy candles, I hope," the principal replied. "I was just filling my office space with Lavender Lift today." When he mentioned the candles, I braced myself. I hoped we wouldn't have to get into *that* right now.

Fernando didn't miss a beat, though. "No, we're talking about a rotten egg smell," he said.

"Oh, that," he replied, with a knowing nod. "That's definitely not coming from my candles.

I have overheard a few students talking about it, though. Why don't you come inside and we'll discuss this some more? We've got to get these folks back to the books," he said, gesturing to the lawn full of students.

"Sounds good to me," I said. The rest of the Crew nodded in agreement. We started walking up toward the school doors. I ran back to the train to get my Can-Man Knapsack. That's where I keep all the gadgets we might need on an investigation. In the rush to check out the gas leak, I'd forgotten it. But I didn't want to go back in there without the masks.

As I jogged across the lawn toward the train, I heard Principal Marsh call out to the students from the front steps. "Attention, students! The gas leak was a false alarm. Please do not let it disturb your inner peace. And do come back inside when you're ready to cope with the math exam again."

From the lawn, I heard the sound of a thousand teenagers groaning.

CHAPTER FOUR

Two Principals

After I picked up my Can-Man knapsack, I ran back into the high school through a side door. As I walked down the hall, past the students filing back into the classrooms, I could still smell that nasty odor. It reminded me of riding in my parents' car along the Rachel Carson Freeway, past all the industrial parks and oil refineries. When the smell came in through the windows, I used to pretend my little brother cut the cheese. He always got really mad. That's why it was fun.

I wondered if whatever was causing the smell at Peak Valley could be somewhere nearby. I took a quick look around the lobby where we were standing. It was the first chance I had to really notice the surroundings, since our original entrance was pretty rushed.

The place looked clean, at least. Nothing to suggest the janitors weren't doing their jobs. I checked a couple of the trash cans. They were practically empty, and didn't smell like, well, whatever that stink was. There weren't any big air vents, either, at least not from what I could see. So I went over to the principal's office to meet up with everyone. When I got there, they were all standing in front of the door. Why hadn't they gone in there yet?

Suddenly I remembered why. The place was still a mess from our little fire-extinguisher incident. Uh-oh. Principal Marsh seemed like a really mellow guy, but I was sure when he saw what PJ did to his office, he'd go ballistic. But what could I do? I couldn't just sneak back out the way I came in (although the thought did cross my mind). So I went over and joined my crew mates at the office door . . .

"Curtis! I'm glad you're here!" Principal Marsh said. "Your fellow Crew members are so polite. They actually wanted to wait for you before we went in and sat down. Isn't that inclusive?" I looked over at Keisha and arched my eyebrow. She nodded her head slightly, as if to admit they were just stalling.

Principal Marsh stepped up to the doorway and started reaching for his keys. I ran in front of him and blocked him like there was a bomb behind the door. "Um, I don't think we need to go in your office, Princip . . . I mean Leslie."

"Yeah," Fernando chimed in. "Why don't we just drop jaw out here?"

"What's this dropping jaw stuff?" the principal replied, crinkling his brow in confusion. I wasn't surprised. I didn't exactly expect the principal to use the same slang Brian was digging up.

But suddenly, Principal Marsh's eyes lit up, as if he understood. "Oh, I get it! You're feeling an invalidating energy from this space."

Now it was my turn to be confused. He explained some more. "You students associate this room—the infamous Principal's Office—with punishment and shame. Well, I can assure you, those are two things I won't tolerate as a leader of this school. From now on, this is an office of big happy smiles. Now please, let me in."

I tried to protest, but it was no use. We couldn't keep the guy out of his own office forever. I slinked aside and looked away as the door creaked open. At first there was silence. Then, a gasp.

"Oh no!" Principal Marsh cried out. "My personal work habitat! It's been ransacked! Vandalized! Destroyed! After all I tried to give to this school!" He started dashing around the office, wiping fire extinguisher foam off all the candles with his sweater. It wasn't doing much good. It looked like somebody had a whipped-cream fight in there.

He sank into his chair, looking depressed. "Maybe the other teachers were right," the principal said. "Maybe eliminating security on campus was a big mistake. I guess we weren't ready for that level of trust as a school community."

"Actually, if it makes you feel any better, we were the ones who did this," PJ admitted.

"What?" Principal Marsh said, looking up. "I don't understand!"

"We saw all the candles, and since we thought there was a gas leak, we were afraid the place might blow up," I explained. "Sorry we made such a mess."

"Oh, I see. I guess the safety of the school was more important than my aromatherapy candles." Principal Marsh sighed. "I'm sorry I got upset with you. It isn't easy to keep your smile on here, you know. Every day it's a new crisis. Sometimes I wish I never accepted this promotion."

"What did you do here before?" Fernando asked.

"I was the football coach," he replied.

"No wonder they never beat anybody," PJ

muttered to me under her breath. I had to stifle a laugh. It was true. Peak Valley once got a mention in *Sports Week* magazine for having the worst high school football team in America. At the time, I think they had lost sixty-eight straight games, including one exhibition game against the nuns at Saint Sylvester's Catholic Academy.

"Why don't we talk about what we came here to talk about?" Keisha asked, flashing a knowing look at the two of us. "What else can you tell us about this weird smell?"

"Well, not a whole lot," the principal replied. "I mean, I smelled it myself for the first time today. A couple of the debate students had complained about smelling it at practice, though. And I heard it hit the basketball team too."

"Huh. We didn't hear about the basketball team," Fernando said. "Are you sure it wasn't just . . . er . . . body odor?"

"You'd have to ask them," Principal Marsh said. "But they've been practicing every day for two weeks, and I never heard about a smell like that before. Couldn't have come at a worse time, either. They're shaping up for the big game against Snurdburg High."

"What about the cafeteria? Have they been serving up a lot of bean burritos lately?" Fernando asked. "Maybe everyone's dropping stealth bombs . . ."

"You just had to go there, didn't you?" I said to him.

"No, no, kids, please! Don't silence your peers. It's a valid question about a natural issue," Principal Marsh replied. "But I'm afraid the answer is no. No beans, no cabbage, no Brussels sprouts. It's a low-gas menu at the cafeteria this week."

"It looks like we're going to keep looking then," Keisha said, jotting down a few more notes. "Is it okay if we hang around for a few days and investigate?"

"Oh, please do!" Principal Marsh replied. "If you can find out the source of this distraction, I'd be elated. There's that state math exam going on right now, and all the Homecoming games are just a couple weeks away. And I'd hate to have anything sapping the students' focus!" He paused for a second, and looked around the room. "Just . . . one thing, please?" he added sheepishly.

"Yeah?" I asked.

"Can you try to respect my office space from now on?"

"Sure thing," I said. With that, we stepped back out into the hall.

By now, most of the kids had filed back inside. I could hear a lot of yelling just around the corner. We all tiptoed over there to see what was going on.

When I peeked around the corner, I saw a tall, skinny kid in rumpled clothes. He was being held hostage by a stern-looking woman with frizzy hair and horn-rimmed glasses. She wasn't big or strong-looking, but her voice alone was enough to scare him stiff.

"Tuck in that shirt, Anderson! Button that collar!" she barked at the boy, tapping a ruler in her hands and circling him like a tiger. "When was your last haircut? Your exiguous grooming habits are a disgrace to this school!"

"Ex . . . excuse me, Principal Snidely?" Anderson asked, his voice trembling nervously. "My *what* grooming habits?"

Principal Snidely? I wondered. *Didn't Brian say she left?* Even if she had, she sure looked like she was in her element.

"EXIGUOUS!" she shrieked. She got right up in his face and slowly mouthed each syllable, like he was deaf. "*Eggs-igg-you-us!* As in skimpy! Pathetically inadequate! In other words, it doesn't cut the mustard! My word, the vocabulary around here gets worse every year!" she muttered.

While she was yelling at him, I noticed the rotten egg smell was getting stronger. *Okay, that's enough,* I thought. *I'm not subjecting myself to this stink when I have technology at my disposal.* I reached into my Can-Man Knapsack and put on my gas mask. I started pulling out everyone else's masks, but nobody looked really eager to suit up.

"Curtis!" PJ hissed. "Give me a break! We don't need those!"

I offered one to Keisha and Fernando. They both shook their heads.

"No, that's fine," Keisha said.

"I'm okay too," Fernando assured me.

I kept the mask on for a second, but I have to admit something about standing in a school hallway wearing a gas mask made me feel, well, a little silly. I didn't end up leaving it on for very long. But it was on long enough to distract Ms. Snidely from her bawl-out session. "My, how ostentatious," she said, glancing up at me.

"Osten-what-sis?" I asked, as I slipped the mask off my head.

"It means showy. An eyesore," Keisha whispered to me. "And that's what it was!"

"Very good, Miss," Principal Snidely said with a smile. "We could use more students like you here."

Just then I heard Principal Marsh's voice behind me. "Excuse me, Zelda?"

"What is it?" Ms. Snidely snapped. Then she recognized Principal Marsh. "Oh, it's *you*," she said, sounding unimpressed.

"Yes, it is me," Principal Marsh said. Even *he* sounded a little nervous. But he tried to be firm. "And I don't want to interrupt your dialogue with Mr. Anderson here, but you know, I *am* principal now." Ms. Snidely didn't respond. "Remember?"

Suddenly Ms. Snidely pasted on a big smile. It looked forced. "Of course I do, Leslie. And I'm sure you're doing a fine job. It's just that I was stopping back in to pick up my beloved ficus plant from my old office, and I got a little nostalgic. I certainly hope you don't misinterpret my brusquerie with this student."

"Brusquerie?" Principal Marsh asked.

"Abruptness of manner. Talking short to him. Old habits die hard, you know."

"Yes, well, maybe it's time to challenge

those old habits," Principal Marsh said. "Why don't you let Mr. Anderson go on his way? After all, you don't need to worry about discipline anymore."

"Certainly, Leslie," Ms. Snidely replied. She turned to Anderson. "You're dismissed!" she snapped. Anderson turned tail and ran like a scared mouse. "I *am* going to miss the little scamps," she said. "But it is refreshing to get into a new line of work. I'll go pick up my plant now. So long, Leslie!" She waved cheerfully and walked away. As she disappeared down the hallway, I saw students get out of her way as if they were playing street hockey and she was a Mack truck.

"Whoa! What's up with *her?*" Fernando asked Principal Marsh, after Ms. Snidely was safely out of earshot.

Principal Marsh looked a little uncomfortable, but he brushed off the question. "Ms. Snidely is just having a little trouble letting go of her old job as principal here," he said. "Hopefully it won't last very long. Now, I know you kids want time to fully embrace your little smell investigation. And as for me, I've got to run off to the candle and incense shop before it closes. So I'll leave you to your detective work for now. Remember, think positive!" With that, he strolled out the front doors.

"Is it just me, or was the smell a lot worse just now?" I asked.

"It's not just you," Fernando said. "I smelled it on that Anderson kid. It must have been soaked into his clothes. He reeked!"

"Maybe the smell's moved to some other part of the school," I said. "I wonder where we should start looking."

Just then Brian came around the corner. "Hey, Curtis, Crew, what's green?"

"What's *green?*" PJ replied. "I don't know. Grass? Month-old tuna?"

Fernando said shook his head. "He means green as in 'what's new,' or 'what's going on?' Right?" Brian nodded in agreement.

"Oh, that. Right," I said. Lucky guess. "Well, for one thing, we just saw your old principal."

Suddenly, Brian's eyes looked like they were ready to pop out of his face. "Snidely? Where? Is she still here?" He started frantically tucking in his shirt and buttoning his top button.

"Don't worry about it, she's gone," Keisha said. "We can see why you'd be a little scared of her, though."

"Scared?" Brian said. Now he was putting on his Cool Guy face. "I'm not scared, I just didn't want to get you guys in trouble." I had to laugh. He knew he wasn't putting that one over on me. "So anyway," he said, trying to change the subject, "did you find out anything about the smell?"

"Well, we know it's not a gas leak," PJ said.

"Right. I got that from the whole going-back-in-the-building thing," Brian said with a smile.

"Other than that, it's back to square one," I told him. "Did you smell it on your way over here?"

"To tell you the truth, I think it's lightening up," Brian replied, sniffing the air once or twice just to be sure.

"Great," Keisha said. "Just when we need it to stink, it goes away."

"Hey, why don't you just come meet me at debate practice tomorrow," Brain offered. "That's where the stink hit the first time. Maybe it'll happen again. Then you can nail it at the source."

"Sounds like a good idea," Fernando said. Then he whispered to me: "Except how exactly are we planning on nailing it?"

"Good question," I muttered back.

We were saved by the bell. "That's my cue for geometry," Brian said. "I guess I'll catch you tomorrow afternoon, then. Click!" He gave us a quick wave. I guess 'click' meant goodbye.

"Yeah, click," I replied. He went through a pair of double doors and disappeared down a stairwell.

"So," Fernando said, "I guess we've got another question to answer. What do we do with this smell once we find it?"

"You mean how do we find out what it is?" Keisha asked.

"Exactly," he replied.

"Let's go back to the Control Car and figure it out," PJ said. "Maybe ALEC will have something for us."

"Sounds like a plan," I said. "Let's go."

As we walked outside, the disappearance of the last traces of the rotten egg smell made a huge difference. I found myself hoping we'd solve the case soon. Too much time up close and personal with this stuff was going to, well, stink.

CHAPTER FIVE

Back on the Train, Gang

The first part of our investigation had pretty much taken us in a big circle. There was no gas leak, which was both good (because the school wasn't in danger) and bad (because it was pretty darn embarrassing for us). No one knew where the smell was coming from, but it seemed to be able to creep through the school and attack just about anywhere. And it seemed to disappear just as mysteriously as it came.

We were planning to meet Brian at debate practice the next day to see if the stink turned up again. But we wanted to make every minute count once we got there. After all,

Peak Valley had a lot of important things to worry about, like the big math test and all the Homecoming stuff next week. They didn't need this rotten smell getting in their way.

We weren't really sure where to start preparing for our showdown with the stench. But there's one place we always start when we don't know where to start: ALEC the computer. So, after we left Peak Valley, we gathered back in the Control Car and fired him up . . .

"Hellllllooooo, Crew! How was the smell?" ALEC asked cheerfully, as his monitor sprang to life.

"It was pretty rank," PJ replied.

"Really?" ALEC said with a curious *bloop*. "Tell me more," he said eagerly. His circuits fluttered in excitement. "Did the sensation hit you when it first wafted up your nose? Or did it take a moment or two to sink in? Was it pungent? Was it sulfurous? Was it earthy? Did it remind you of long-lost, faraway places?"

"ALEC!" Keisha said, giggling. "It just stank! What are you getting so worked up about?"

ALEC let out something that sounded like a sigh. "Oh, I'm sorry, Keisha. Whenever I hear about human senses, I get so, well, envious. I wish I could experience the perfume of a rose, or the allure of a freshly baked pizza."

"But ALEC," I protested, "what do you have to complain about? You've got the most sophisticated sensors around!"

"Ah, yes, but they still can't match the human senses. Your eyes, nose, ears, tongue, and skin are incredibly complex analytical tools! Take your olfactory system . . ."

"Our what?" Fernando interrupted.

"Olfactory system. A fancy word for your sense of smell," ALEC explained. "It's the oldest and, in some ways, the most complex of the human senses. With it, you humans can identify hundreds, or sometimes even thousands, of different odors!"

"Wow. I never knew our noses were so sensitive," Keisha said thoughtfully.

I have to admit, I found myself suddenly sniffing the air in the Control Car, to see what I could pick out. I could smell the alcohol I use for cleaning ALEC's hardware, the fancy shampoo Keisha uses in her hair, and a trace of the submarine sandwich PJ had for lunch. I couldn't figure out where that was coming from, until I noticed the wrapper in the open wastebasket.

Meanwhile, ALEC was still going on about smell. "And if you think *your* noses are sensitive, just imagine what it's like to be a dog!" he continued, almost dreamily. "A dog nose is hundreds of times more sensitive than a human nose. In fact, animals like dogs and mice can even recognize each other by their smell!"

"I can think of a couple guys in my class that I can recognize by their smell," Fernando said.

"Okay, I don't think we need any more details on *that*," Keisha said, getting back down to business. "What we do need to know is how to put these noses of ours to use. We've got to go back to Peak Valley and find out what that rotten egg smell is."

"Have you identified the source?" ALEC asked.

"Negative," I replied. "It wasn't a gas leak. Peak Valley High doesn't use gas."

ALEC let out an apologetic *blorp*. "Sorry, Curtis," he said. "Hope I didn't cause any trouble."

"Well, luckily, it doesn't look like anyone can get in trouble over there, as long as Leslie's in charge," Fernando said with a smirk. He had a point. That guy was about as tough as a melted marshmallow.

"We might be able to find out where it's coming from tomorrow, ALEC," PJ said. "But what if we can't? What if we just smell it again, and can't figure out where it's coming from?"

"PJ's right," I said. "We haven't been able to find the source so far."

"Maybe I can help!" ALEC offered. His monitor glowed brightly with anticipation. "I may not have the nose for news that you kids have, but I *do* have a mass spectrometer!"

"Great!" PJ said. Then she stopped. "What's a mass spectrometer?"

"A mass spectrometer is a kind of mechanical nose—it's used to identify gases. It works by isolating a small sample of the gas, and then bombarding that sample with lasers or electron beams."

"Cool!" I said. I looked over at Fernando, PJ, and Keisha. They didn't look as enthusiastic. Fernando was zoning out, Keisha was smiling politely, and PJ had actually wandered over to the back of the Control Car. Sometimes I can't believe that my own Crew mates have no appreciation for hard-core technology.

ALEC seemed more than happy to keep talking, though. "When the gas molecules get hit with lasers," he went on, "they get broken down into electrically charged pieces called ions. By manipulating those ions in a magnetic field, I can identify them and therefore also identify the gas in question!"

As ALEC yammered on with excitement, Fernando held up his hand to get a word in. "One question, ALEC," he said. "The smell is at Peak Valley High. You're here. So how do we get the stink into this mass spectrometer of yours?"

Before ALEC could answer, PJ called to us from the back of the Control Car. "Hey!" she said. "Why don't we just use Zorro?" She pressed a button and a small panel, kind of like a doggie-door, opened up at the bottom of the far wall. With a digitized yelp, Zorro scurried out from behind the panel and into the Control Car. Her metal fur glinted under the harsh fluorescent lights.

Zorro is the latest addition to the Super Crew. She's not human, and she can't talk like ALEC, but she's still pretty amazing in her own way. She's a little robot that Dr. Alexander Graham Cracker gave us to help us on our cases. She's named after the animal she looks like: the common South American zorro (it looks kind of like a dog, but it's really a species of fox). And she's specially designed for rooting around in places humans can't get to, retrieving small objects, and analyzing chemicals—like smells. Perfect! I couldn't believe I didn't think of bringing her in myself. I guess I kinda got caught up in ALEC's techno-talk.

"Oh, no!" ALEC whined when he realized Zorro was out and about. "You're not going to rely on that little bag of bolts, are you? Someone might step on it!"

I forgot to mention something else. See, ALEC and Zorro have a little sibling-rivalry thing going. Personally, I don't think ALEC has any reason to be jealous. After all, his artificial intelligence system is one of the best in the world, and Zorro can only follow simple voice commands. But I guess when you're used to being top dog, even a little competition can be scary. Plus, ALEC's always wished he could move around.

"Come on, ALEC!" Keisha said. "Zorro's perfect for this job! She'll track down the source of that smell in no time!"

"Hmpf!" ALEC replied. "This is a job for a world-class supercomputer, not some little tin dog!"

I heard a *whirr* from Zorro. I looked down and saw a little piece of ticker tape roll out of her "mouth." That's how she tells us things. I bent down and tore off the tape to read it.

"I am not a dog. I am a South American common zorro. It's a species of fox," the tape read. Zorro had her sensitive side too, I guess.

"Come on, ALEC," PJ pleaded. "Zorro can tell us what that smell is. That's exactly what she's designed for."

"You did say that dogs have the best noses," Fernando added. Zorro spat out another piece of tape. He picked it up and read it.

"What's it say?" Keisha asked.

"I am not a dog. I am a South American common zorro . . ." Fernando read aloud.

"We know, we know!" ALEC said sharply. "Look, Crew, I know Zorro can identify a few chemicals. But she just can't hold up to the power of my mass spectrometer. And besides,

Dr. Cracker hasn't even worked all the bugs out of her hardware yet!"

ALEC had a point there. Zorro did have a few behavior problems. Once we took her on a case out at Fairhaven Park and she dug up all the flower beds in a one-mile area. She also had a bad habit of jumping on people and trying to analyze the chemistry of their clothes. When she did that to the Mayor's mother, she almost fell over from shock.

"Okay, I've got a plan," I said. "We'll take Zorro out to Peak Valley, but we'll collect some of the smell for ALEC, too, just in case anything goes wrong."

"And to confirm the robot's highly questionable results!" ALEC insisted.

"Sure, whatever," I said. Anything to stop him from bickering.

"So how do we bring the smell back to ALEC?" PJ asked.

"Simple, PJ!" ALEC replied. With a short *whirr*, a small drawer on the lower part of his control panel opened up. There was a little glass vial inside of it. It looked kind of like the ones doctors use to take blood samples. *Ugh.* Just the thought of that made me a little queasy.

"When you smell the stink, just go up to the stinkiest place in the room and hold this vial open. Give it a couple seconds, and then seal it up tight. Then bring it back here immediately, and I'll analyze it. The vial's airtight, so the smelly chemical should stay right inside."

"Sounds good," Fernando said. "We'll sic Zorro on that smell tomorrow, and we'll save some gas for ALEC too."

Zorro yelped happily. It sounded almost like a bark, but not quite. PJ patted Zorro's wiry fur. "You ready for a big day tomorrow, pooch?" she asked. "Think you can track down this nasty smell?"

A light went on in Zorro's "eyes," and after another quick *whirr*, a piece of ticker tape tumbled out of her. PJ ripped it off and read it.

"Well? What does she have to say?" Keisha asked.

"I am not a 'pooch.' I am a South American common zorro. It's a species of fox," PJ read from the tape.

I had a feeling tomorrow was going to be a rough day.

CHAPTER SIX

The Stink Strikes Again

We arrived at Peak Valley High after school the following day, ready for phase two of our investigation. We were meeting Brian at debate practice in the cafeteria, where the smell had first attacked. Keisha was carrying the little glass vial ALEC had given us. Zorro trotted along behind us in her jerky little robotic way. Her "feet" were actually little treads, like on a tank, so she wasn't exactly graceful.

We went around to the back of the building and walked down a flight of stairs to the basement, where the cafeteria was. When we opened the basement door, we ran into a *funny little man with a handlebar mustache who was on his way out. And I mean we literally ran into him—we knocked him right over, and a couple of empty crates he was carrying tumbled out of his arms and across the floor. As if that wasn't enough, Zorro sprang to life and started jumping all over him . . .*

"Oof! What is this?" the main muttered, in what sounded like a French accent. "Get this strange creature off of me at once!"

"Bad Zorro! Bad Zorro!" Keisha shouted. That was Zorro's cue to stop whatever she was doing. At least she obeyed it. She rolled right off the guy on her little tank-tread feet and plopped back onto the ground.

"What on earth is that?" the man asked, as he struggled back to his feet.

"Um, that's just our science project," I explained. "It's an automatic newspaper fetcher. It doesn't really work right." In situations like this, I feel like it's better not to explain any more than you have to. Otherwise, you could spend the whole day explaining.

"Really?" the man replied, arching an eyebrow at Zorro. Luckily, Zorro was doing her best at looking dumb. She just sat there. He nodded at her and began to dust himself off.

"We're really sorry," Keisha said politely.

"It's okay. I have felt worse," the man said. He picked up one of the crates that he had been carrying. It was marked *Teen Fresh*. "So, how are you kids enjoying our free gifts?" he asked, putting on a friendlier face.

We had no idea what he was talking about. "I don't think we've gotten any," Fernando said.

"You haven't? I thought everyone in the school was supposed to!" he exclaimed.

Now I was really confused. So was everyone else. "We're not actually students here. We go to Kinetic City," Keisha explained.

"Oh. Never mind, then. My mistake," the man said, and walked past us. "*Au revoir!*" he said cheerfully as he left. "Good luck with your little science doggy!"

I heard a *whirr* and saw a ticker tape roll out of Zorro's mouth. I saw the words "I am not a dog" and decided not to read any more of it.

"I wonder what gifts he was talking about," Fernando said, as we stepped inside and walked down toward the cafeteria doors.

"Beats me," said PJ. There was no time to try and figure it out, though. We had reached the cafeteria doors, and the start of our mission. We swung the doors open and went inside, with Zorro toddling behind us.

The first thing I noticed was a smell. The distinctive smell of . . . *vanilla*. Although it didn't help us with the case, it was definitely a pleasant surprise.

"Mmmm . . . smell that!" Keisha said as we went in. "They must have made cookies in here today."

"Yeah, I wish we could get their cooks to work at *our* cafeteria," Fernando said.

The cafeteria looked pretty normal. I didn't see anything offhand that looked like the source of a stink—no open garbage, no big air vents. It looked a lot like our cafeteria at Kinetic City High. I even noticed a few posters up about study skills, bike safety, and nutrition. We had those same sort of public-service ads at our school too. Except theirs all had that "Teen Fresh" logo in the upper right-hand corner—the same logo that was on the crate the French guy was carrying. Maybe that's what he was talking about. He must have been delivering those posters. He was probably giving some out to the Peak Valley kids to take home.

Brian was at a table over by the back door. About a dozen other debaters were with him. He saw us and waved us over. Today he was wearing all white, and his hair was tied into little knots.

"Hey, you're just in time. Come on over and leave it somewhere," Brian said. I assumed he meant "sit down," so we did.

"So far, so good, huh?" I asked. "I mean, I don't smell anything nasty."

"The afternoon's young, Curtis," he replied. "It took a while to hit at the last practice too." He noticed what everyone else in the room was already staring at: Zorro. "What's *that?*" he asked.

"That's Zorro," PJ explained proudly. "She's our robot assistant. She'll help us find the smell. But we'd better keep her quiet until then."

"I'll take your word for it," Brian said. He gestured toward his teammates around the table. "Super Crew, meet the Peak Valley Monsters of Debate. Everyone, this is the Kinetic City Super Crew and their, um . . . zorro. They're here to check out that righteously sweet egg smell." His teammates nodded and smiled in approval. I guess they were used to Brian's weird language.

"So what do we do?" PJ asked.

"I guess we just hang out here until the smell hits," I replied.

"Sounds like a plan to me. We're gonna start practice. Hopefully we'll be interesting enough to keep you awake," Brian said. Then he turned to his teammates to psych them up. "Okay, all, here we go. Who's the best?"

"WE ARE!!!!" everyone shouted.

"And who are we gonna beat?" Brian said, louder than before.

"SNURDBURG!!!!" they shouted back.

"You're debating against Snurdburg?" PJ asked. She turned to Fernando. "Didn't Principal Marsh say they were playing them in basketball too?"

"I thought so," Fernando said.

"We're playing Snurdburg in everything next weekend—basketball, football, debate, chess, you name it," Brian explained. "It's a Homecoming tradition. They're our arch-rivals."

"And they're totally obnoxious," one of his teammates added.

"Yeah, last year they spray-painted 'Peak Valley Bites' on the football field the night before the big game," said a tall kid next to Brian.

"And the year before they stole the Peak Valley Wombat and wrapped him in toilet paper!" a girl at the end of the table said, jumping in.

"The Peak Valley *Wombat?*" PJ asked.

"It's our mascot. It's just a costume," Brian explained.

"But your mascot is a *wombat?*" PJ said in disbelief.

"Yeah, it used to be a wildcat, but Snurdburg threw our wildcat costume in a nuclear waste dump three years ago," Brian replied. "The wombat was all they had at the costume outlet to replace it."

"Oh," PJ said, backing off. Those Snurdburg kids sounded like some real wastes of space.

The girl at the end spoke up again. "But those Snurdburgers can do whatever they want. We're still going to kick their cans next weekend. Right?"

"YEAH!!!" the team replied. You had to admire their spirit.

"Okay, let's get down to it," Brian said. He was the team captain, so he ran the show. "We'll start with this proposal: Peak Valley should turn the big parking lot off Franklin Boulevard into a park, and then blacktop over Adams Park and turn it into a parking lot. Gwen, you take 'pro.' Luis, you're 'con.' Let's go!"

Gwen, the girl at the end of the table, got up and started off her argument in favor of the proposal. That's what you do in debating: you take some suggestion or idea, and then one person argues for it ('pro') and the other against it ('con'). Whoever makes the best argument, according to the judges, wins.

Personally, I didn't really care. Debating isn't really my thing. It's all about stuff that isn't really going to happen anyway. I'd rather have my hands right in something, like a computer CPU or my inventions (my favorite is the Snake-Net-Sling-o-Matic, which has caught us a few real snakes and a couple of snake-like bad guys).

Keisha seemed interested, though. She likes ideas, and working things through. Her favorite subject is history, and she had just done a report on the famous presidential debates between Abraham Lincoln and Stephen Douglas. So she sat up close to the debaters, keeping her eyes wide open, nodding when she agreed with something, and writing things down in her notebook when it looked like she didn't agree.

Meanwhile, Fernando and PJ just sort of hung back and kept quiet. As for me, I started to doze off. In fact, I must have been out for at least half an hour, because when I woke up, everyone was shouting.

"You call that a rebuttal?" Brian was yelling at another kid, the tall boy who had been sitting next to Brian earlier. He and another girl had taken the place of Gwen and Luis. They must have moved on to another topic. "Come on, man, I've seen you do ten times better!"

The tall kid wiped his forehead and unbuttoned his collar. "Give me a break, Brian, I'm doing my best. How do you argue *for* giving free cigarettes to freshmen? Can't you just back off a little?"

"Back off?" Brian shot back. "Is Snurdburg going to back off? I don't think so! You've got to be able to argue *for* any idiot thing, or *against* the best idea in the world! If not, they're going to house us this weekend!"

"*House* us?" the girl asked quizzically.

"Kick our behinds!" Brian explained. Then he rubbed his temples and turned to the girl. "It's our fault too! You and I could have dug up better facts today."

"Come on, Brian, we did the best we could!" she said, looking frustrated. "We both spent three hours in the library looking this stuff up, remember?"

"Well, maybe that's not enough!" Brian said. He was really getting worked up. He turned to his teammates. "Come on, people, this is hard, but we've got to pull together here. We've got to be ready for whatever Snurdburg dishes out. We can't disgrace ourselves in front of those morons!"

Luis, the guy from the first debate, stood up in protest. "But we've only got so much time. What about homework?"

Gwen, the girl who had debated with Luis, chimed in. "Yeah, and we've got that math exam all week! It's just too much!"

His teammates raised their voices in agreement. It was turning into a debate for the debaters. And just as the tension was peaking, my nostrils quivered. There it was. The rotten egg smell. It settled over us like a low-lying stink cloud. Everyone was coughing and trying to fan the smell away. It wasn't working.

"Oh, man, who cut the cheese?" Fernando said, covering his nose with his sweater.

"That's gotta be one big cheese," Keisha replied, waving her hand in front of her face.

It was time to unleash our robot assistant. "Come on, Zorro! Find the smell!" PJ commanded.

With a quick jerk, Zorro sprang to life and wagged her little wire tail. She started circling around the room, whirring and clicking all the way. Within a minute or so, she started hovering around the debater's table.

"That's weird," Fernando said. "What's Zorro doing over by the debate table? Where does she think the smell's coming from?"

Just then, the debater named Gwen made a big mistake. She had obviously had enough of the smell, and stood up to leave. Unfortunately, when she did that, she got right in Zorro's way. The little robot pounced on her enthusiastically. Gwen fell backward from the sheer shock, and Zorro began frantically tramping all over her.

"Help! Somebody stop this thing!" Gwen yelled. It was probably her first time getting stomped on by a robot zorro, and she definitely wasn't enjoying it.

Keisha ran over to rescue her. "Stop! Bad Zorro! *Bad Zorro!*" she scolded. Zorro heeded her command, shut herself off, and plonked to the floor.

"You might want to get a leash for that," Gwen said as she stood up and brushed off her blazer.

"Yeah, that's a good idea," Keisha said, glaring at the motionless Zorro. She picked up the robot and handed it to PJ. "Here, PJ, make sure Zorro stays off. She's getting a little too frisky. I'll just grab some of the smell in that test tube ALEC gave us." PJ nodded and cradled Zorro in her arms. She looked a little disappointed.

Meanwhile, Keisha reached into her pocket and pulled out the vial we got from ALEC. She opened it, waved it through the smelly air, and then sealed it tight. "Gotcha!" she said triumphantly, slipping the stink-filled vial back in her pocket.

"Great. Now let's get out of here!" I said. "I can't take this anymore!"

I was really just talking to the rest of the Crew, but the whole debate team decided it was time to leave too. We all ran out the way we came in, down the corridor and out the back door into the open air. The smell lifted and we breathed a sigh of relief. The debaters all went their separate ways, but Brian caught up with us.

"Man, that was worse than ever!" he said. "And it's clinging to me again!" He waved his arms around to air out his shirt. "I might have to take out my hair knots just to ventilate my head." He started untying the little knots in his hair as we walked away from the school.

"Well, we got our sample, so we should be able to find out what this smell is," I told him. "But I still don't know how it's getting to you."

"If somebody's bringing it in, they've gotta be pretty sneaky," Keisha said. "They slipped that stuff in right under our noses!" She snorted at her own pun. "Get it?"

The rest of us just exchanged tired looks. That's about all you can do when Keisha gets her humor bug.

As we circled around toward the other side of the building, we ran into a lanky guy in a basketball uniform.

"Hey, Chad," Brian said, slapping his hand.

"Hey," Chad replied. Before he could get any further, he noticed Zorro in PJ's arms. "What's *that?*" he asked.

"Science project," I jumped in. "Fancy toaster. It brings the toast to you."

"Huh," Chad said, looking a little confused. "That's cool, I guess."

Thankfully, Brian changed the subject. "So, what's green?" he asked. "Practice let out early?"

"Yeah," Chad replied. "We stunk."

"Stunk as in you were good, right?" Fernando asked. Brian shook his head 'no.' I guess he could tell when someone was being serious.

"No, I mean we really stunk," said Chad. "That nasty rotten egg smell hit us again. We had to stop after twenty minutes. If this keeps up, we'll never be ready for Snurdburg next weekend."

Just then we heard a voice yell out from near the street alongside us. "PEAK VALLEY BITES!" it said.

We turned and saw another high school boy with a hat pulled down over his forehead, baggy jeans, and a denim jacket with a big "S" on the lapel. He was walking a mountain bike along the sidewalk.

"Get out of here, Snurdface!" Chad yelled back. "You're going down next Saturday!"

"Yeah, keep talking, Geek Valley!" the kid replied. "We're gonna do a number on you just like every year. And don't go crying to your mom when we do it! See you on the court!" With that, he hopped on his bike and sped off.

We had to hold PJ back from going after him. "Hey, get back here!" she yelled. "Why don't you step a little closer and say that!" PJ's a tough kid for her size, but she can get a little carried away.

"Don't worry about it," Brian said. "They're losers. Let them talk if they want. Words can't hurt us." He stopped and thought for a second. "Well, except in the debate tournament, I guess." Then he looked a little depressed.

"Yeah, and they're gonna wipe us up on the b-ball court if this smell keeps up," Chad said. He sounded pretty down too. He slapped Brian on the shoulder halfheartedly. "I'll catch you later, Brian," he muttered. Then he shuffled off with his head hung low.

We continued around the corner, toward the front of the school. I decided to say what I could tell everyone else was thinking. "This smell is looking less and less like a natural accident," I said.

"You said it," Fernando agreed. "Just look at who it's hitting. The basketball team. The debate team. Brian's band."

"And they're all key players in the Homecoming events," Keisha noted. "Someone wants Peak Valley to fail in everything they try—to stink! And who wants that more than anybody?"

"Snurdburg!" we all said, pretty much at once.

"You're right," Brian said. "Those jerks! This is their worst prank ever!"

"And it's only the beginning," PJ said, pointing across the front parking lot.

I looked over. She was pointing at the sign in the front of the school. It was one of those big signs with magnetic letters. Earlier today it had said THE FIRST SCHOOL PLAY STARTS IN TWO WEEKS! But someone had taken away a bunch of the letters. Now it said

TH I S SCHOOL   ST   IN   KS!

"No question," Fernando said. "I smell a rat."

"A Snurdburg rat," Brian added.

"Come on, Crew, let's get back and analyze this sample," Keisha said. "Then we'll come back and set ourselves a rat trap!"

CHAPTER SEVEN

Unnatural Gas

We rushed back from Peak Valley High School to the Control Car of the KC Express train, with the deactivated Zorro in PJ's arms and a little tube of stink gas in Keisha's pocket. We were almost positive that some kids from Snurdburg were behind the stink epidemic at Peak Valley. After all, they had the strongest motive we knew of--and a love of obnoxious pranks to go with it. The question was, how were they doing it?

To answer that, our first step was to have ALEC analyze the gas sample from the cafeteria. If we knew what the stink was made of, that might help us unravel Snurdburg's secret plan. As soon as we got into the Control Car, we flipped ALEC on for *assistance. I figured he'd be pretty happy to hear about our little problem with Zorro . . .*

"Helllllloooooo, Crew!" ALEC exclaimed as his circuits fired up. "I was just interfacing with a computer over at Tufts University in Massachusetts. Did you know they're working on an artificial nose over there? It can tell gases apart with fiber-optic sensors, that act a lot like the nerve cells in your own nose! Maybe someday, I'll have a sniffer to rival yours after all!"

"Well, for now, the one you've got is good enough," PJ said, setting Zorro down in the corner. "Zorro didn't get a chance to analyze the smell."

"I knew it!" ALEC said excitedly, in his I-told-you-so tone. "Never take a chance on untested technology! I had a feeling that little mutt wasn't up to the challenge!"

"Okay, okay, you were right!" Fernando said, cutting him off. "Just open up your lab port so we can give you the gas sample!"

With a short *whirr*, ALEC's lab port slid out from his control panel. Keisha reached into her pocket and pulled out the little glass tube full of the mystery stench. She clamped it onto a prong inside the port and pushed the button to close the port.

"Okay, ALEC, let her rip!" she said. "Show us what this stuff's made of!"

"Right away, Keisha!" ALEC gurgled happily. If there's one thing you can say for ALEC, it's that he's always glad to be of service. "Commencing mass spectrometry sequence now!"

The analysis took up some major juice. The Control Car lights dimmed as ALEC let his lasers go to town on our little gas sample. If I didn't know him better, I'd have worried that ALEC was going to overload his circuits. But he's not the self-destructive type.

After a few second's ALEC's monitor went black, and then a bunch of sharp, spiky vertical lines popped up across it. It looked sort of like those bar graphs you do in math class, except the bars were really skinny, and spaced out kind of funny. Another weird thing was that most of them were either tiny or huge.

I had to ask about it. I can't just not know what's going on. "What's that stuff on your screen, ALEC?"

His voice came back a little garbled because we were already using up so much memory. But I could understand him. "That's the mass spectrogram of the sample!" he said excitedly. "Each of those spikes represents a kind of charged particle that broke off when I hit the gas with the lasers. The bigger the spike, the more of that particle there is."

"Cool," I said.

"Get to the point," Fernando said.

"Certainly, Fernando!" ALEC replied. "First, I'll just factor out the spectrogram of regular air." With a *bloop*, a couple of the big spikes disappeared from the monitor. "Then I'll match this spectrogram to the ones of known chemicals in my files," ALEC continued. "Every chemical has its own spectrogram, you know. Once we've got a match, we'll know what you're looking at. Checking . . ." ALEC whirred and beeped for a few more seconds, and then let out a triumphant DING!

"Matched and finished!" he exclaimed.

"What've you got?" Fernando asked. "Is it rotten eggs? Moldy cheese?"

"Negative, Fernando!" ALEC replied. "It's a synthetic mercaptan!"

"Mercaptan, huh?" I repeated. "Where did I hear that before?"

"From ALEC, the other day," Keisha said. "He said it's the smelly stuff they put in natural gas, right?"

"Exactly, Keisha!" ALEC confirmed. "Although some mercaptans occur in nature, too."

"But you said this one's synthetic, right?" I asked. "As in, artificial?"

"Yes, synthetic as in artificial! Man-made! Not occurring in nature!" ALEC replied insistently.

"Well, *that's* weird," Keisha said thoughtfully. "I figured those Snurdburg kids would just use something they found in the trash. How did they get their hands on synthetic mercaptans?"

"I don't know," I said. "But don't underestimate them. They *are* sneaky. Remember, they got the smell into the cafeteria this afternoon and none of us even saw them do it. We're talking about a school where pranks like this are an art form."

"Maybe one of their parents works in a chemical plant," Fernando suggested. "They could have snuck in and siphoned off some mercaptans from the factory pipes."

"Why go through all that trouble? Maybe they just used a stink bomb," PJ offered.

"Great idea, PJ!" I said. I was a little embarrassed that it didn't come up first. Sometimes we work so hard to solve our cases that we overlook the most obvious solutions.

Fernando agreed. "Duh—I can't believe I didn't think of it," he said. "Stink bombs have to use something to make them stink. And I'll bet sometimes it's synthetic mercaptans. I mean, what are they going to do, put rotten eggs in there?"

"Okay, so it might be a stink bomb," Keisha said. "The question is, how do we catch those Snurdburg creeps using it?"

"Well, Brian's band is practicing after school tomorrow," I suggested. "They got stink-attacked earlier this week. And since they're playing at the Homecoming dance, they might be on the hit list for a repeat visit."

"All right, then, we do what we did today," Keisha said.

"Can we bring Zorro?" PJ asked. She looked over at the little robot with puppy-dog eyes. I think she was getting a little too attached.

"I don't know," Fernando said. "That thing's been more trouble than it's worth so far."

"But she can track down the smell!" PJ insisted. "I'm sure she can! I'll keep an eye on her, I promise."

I thought about it for a second. We weren't having much luck tracking down the smell on our own. Maybe Zorro was our best shot. Maybe I could tinker with her a little and get her bad habits under control.

"Okay, fine," I conceded. "I'll work on Zorro tonight and see if I can debug her a little. But if she starts jumping on people tomorrow, we've got to shut her down again."

"Unless it's one of those Snurdburg creeps," PJ said. "I'd love to see Zorro walk right over that kid we saw today."

I smiled. When cases got tough, it was great to have PJ's energy. And we were going to need all the energy we could get. In less than twenty-four hours, we had to prepare for a showdown.

CHAPTER EIGHT

Smells Like Teen Fresh

I stayed up pretty late giving Zorro a technical check-up. I ended up taking her apart and putting her back together again. I'm glad PJ wasn't around to see it. I did spot a couple of loose wires, which might have explained her tendency to jump all over people. Hopefully now that I'd fixed them, she'd be on her best behavior.

We had Zorro with us again when we went to the band room the next afternoon. Brian's band, Bucket, was getting ready to rehearse for the Homecoming dance. We made sure to get there a little early, so we could give the place a thorough inspection before practice started.

The band room had only two doorways. One opened directly to the outside, toward the back parking lot. The other led to a corridor that took you into the rest of the building. With four Crew members on hand, it was going to be pretty easy to keep both doors covered. For now, Fernando and PJ (with Zorro) were standing guard. Meanwhile, just to make sure there weren't any stink bombs pre-planted, Keisha and I searched the place top to bottom. We didn't want to get caught off-guard like last time, so we left no stone unturned . . ..

"Okay, the practice rooms are clear," I said, stepping out of the last of the boxy little rooms that lined one wall of the band room. "No way in or out except from right here in the band room, and nothing in there but music stands."

"And I've checked all the air vents. They're all stink-free. Did you look *inside* the music stands?" Keisha called from the other side of the room, where she was rummaging through the music library.

"Sure did," I said. "They're hollow and odorless!"

Keisha stepped away from the shelves of sheet music, and brushed her hands. "Nothing in there but marches and concertos," she said. "Of course, I can't be sure that none of *them* stink." She giggled to herself. I just smiled politely.

Meanwhile, the band was setting up. Brian was tuning his bass and adjusting the light bulb around his neck. The keyboard player, a redheaded kid named Ross, was trying out all the sound settings on his machine. Some sounded like strings, some like human voices, and some like jackhammers pounding on a rubber sidewalk. Marisa, the drummer, was tapping her sticks nervously on just about everything but her drums—music stands, tables, chairs, even her own knees.

Suddenly, I heard some commotion from the inside door. PJ was talking tough to a short, muscular kid in a tank-top shirt. He was carrying a big black case. He kept trying to get past her, but she blocked him at every turn like a pro linebacker. She held Zorro out in his face threateningly.

"Keep back," she said, "or I'll sic Zorro on you!"

The kid looked at Zorro and snickered. "You think I'm scared of that lunch box?"

A piece of ticker tape scrolled out of Zorro's mouth. The kid with the black case looked surprised, and then gingerly pulled the tape out and read it.

"I am not a lunch box," he read aloud from the slip of paper. "I am a South American common zorro. It's a species of fox . . ."

"That's right! And as far as I can tell, *you're* not a guitar player!" PJ said. "So beat it!"

The boy rolled his eyes impatiently and tossed Zorro's ticker tape aside. "Okay, fine," he said. "You want to see my guitar? Here." He set the black case on the ground, and opened it up. Inside was a sleek red electric guitar. "You satisfied?"

She wasn't. "Nice try. How do I know that's a real guitar and not a stink bomb in disguise?"

The kid threw up his hands in frustration. Luckily, by now Brian had noticed what was going on. He stepped over and got between them.

"It's all right, PJ. This is Jerome, our guitarist. And this guy is ugly."

"Well, *that's* not very nice," PJ said. She set Zorro down cautiously beside her.

"Ugly as in 'like a monster.' In other words, really good," Jerome assured her. *Another speaker of Brianese*, I thought to myself. Then Jerome looked at Brian expectantly and said "Right?"

"Of course," Brian replied. "You know I wouldn't say you were *ugly* ugly. At least not to your face," he said jokingly, giving Jerome a friendly punch on the arm.

"Yeah, just watch it or I'll knock your lights out," Jerome joked back, pointing at the light bulb around Brian's neck. They definitely traded insults like only good friends could. He walked with Brian back to where Ross and Marisa were setting up.

"It looks like we're all clear, Brian," I told him when they settled back in. "Any stink that comes into this room today has to get past us. We'll keep an eye out while you rehearse."

"Great," Brian said. "We can't afford to lose any more time. We've got ten new songs to work on and we're not planning on looking like goofballs when we play at the dance." Then he turned to his band mates. "Everyone ready? Let's start with 'Dead Purple Dinosaur.' One, two, three . . ."

When the band kicked in, the sound was absolutely deafening. I didn't know what kind of music it was, but it sure was noisy. I covered my ears a little. Keisha bobbed her head up and down to the rhythm. She seemed really into it. Amazing.

The important thing was we were covering the doorways. I crouched down by the door to the outside, leaving just a crack for me to see through. Keisha was within an arm's reach, ready to provide reinforcement. On the opposite side of the room, Fernando, PJ, and Zorro hid in the shadows near the inside door, keeping an eye out for intruders.

For a while, nothing happened. Then the band, who had started off good, at least as far as I could tell, started to mess up a lot. Marisa would speed up, Jerome and Ross would come in at the wrong time, and Brian would just start playing the wrong thing altogether. They had started a song called 'Twenty-First Century Slime' over again for the third time when Brian stopped playing and whistled the band to a halt.

"Okay, that's it. I can't take this any more! Jerome, you stink!"

"Hey, man, I was all over that last take," Jerome protested.

"No, I mean, you *stink!*" Brian shot back, waving his hand in front of his nose. "As in reek! As in that nasty smell is back and it's coming from *you!*"

Jerome sniffed the air, winced, and then leaned in toward Brian. He backed off almost instantly. "I hate to say it, bud, but he who smelt it dealt it. That stink is *your* masterpiece, not mine."

"Hold on a second!" I said. "PJ, bring Zorro over here! She'll figure out where this stink is coming from." I could barely smell it myself. Then I took a step closer to the band. It got worse.

"I think it's Ross!" Marisa said from behind her drum kit. I'm smelling it too and I'm closest to him!"

"Hey, don't look at me," Ross said. "This smell's been driving me crazy too. You know the real source? It's Marisa. She's at ground zero."

By now, PJ had brought Zorro over. The little dog—I mean, zorro—was ready for action.

"Okay, folks, this is our robot, Zorro," Keisha said, giving the best explanation she could. "She's trained to sniff out smells. We're going to let her loose and have her figure out where the smell's coming from."

The band members all nodded in agreement between coughs. I think they would have agreed to anything at that point. We were all a little worried about Zorro—even PJ—but she went ahead and gave her the command.

"Go for it, Zorro! Find the stink!"

In no time flat, Zorro pounced right on Brian's chest. Brian managed to keep his footing, but our little metal pet kept hounding him like he had a pocket full of Robot Zorro Treats. *So much for my little repair job*, I thought.

"Oh, no!" PJ said. "Not again!"

I guess it was time to put Zorro to bed. I called over to her: "Bad Zor . . ."

"Hold on!" Keisha said. "Let's not give up on her yet. Maybe there's a reason she's jumping all over everybody."

"Well, it's not me," Brian said, fending off Zorro as she jumped at his heels.

"Just humor me, Brian," Keisha pleaded. "Pick Zorro up and let her take a few readings."

"On me?" he said. "You've got to be kidding."

"Come on, Brian," I urged him. "We've got to try and figure this thing out."

Brian sighed, and reluctantly picked Zorro up. Her wire tail wagged back and forth as she sampled the air. As she rooted around Brian's sweater, he couldn't help laughing.

"Okay, stop! That tickles!"

Suddenly, Zorro seemed satisfied and jumped back down to the floor. Another piece of ticker tape spilled out of her "mouth." I walked over and tore it off.

"What's it say?" Fernando asked.

"Chemical: Synthetic mercaptan gas," I read. "Source: Acrylic sweater. Underarm section."

The entire band, and even the rest of the Crew, burst out laughing. Especially Jerome.

"There you go, Brian. It's you!" Jerome said. He sat down on the floor to catch his breath. Zorro took the opportunity to hop over and plop in Jerome's lap like a happy puppy.

This is weird, I thought. *If the gas is artificial, how can it be coming from Brian?*

That question didn't seem to bother anyone else, though. They were still having a good laugh at Brian's expense. Meanwhile, Brian was looking really embarrassed. "What's the matter, buddy?" Jerome teased. "You forget your Teen Fresh today?"

"No way, man," he said. "This dog's got to be broken!"

Whirr! Another piece of ticker tape came out of Zorro's "mouth." Fernando walked over to Jerome, who was scratching Zorro's shiny head, to get it.

"I know, I know, Zorro, you're not a dog . . ." Fernando said, reaching down to tear off the tape. But when he got a look at what the message said, his expression turned to one of surprise. He read it out loud. "Chemical: Synthetic mercaptan. Source: Human underarm."

There was another laugh from the band (except Jerome), then another *whirr* and another piece of tape from Zorro. Fernando picked it up eagerly and looked at it. "P.S. I am not a dog . . ." he read, before tossing it away.

"Okay, there's got to be some explanation for this," Keisha said, shaking her head in confusion.

"I'll tell you the explanation," said Jerome. "This pooch of yours is totally messed up. I just put on extra Teen Fresh right after gym class."

"Wait a second," Fernando said, taking a step closer to the band. "What's this Teen Fresh stuff you keep talking about?"

"It's this new underarm deodorant," Brian explained. "They're test marketing it here. So they're giving out free samples of it to everybody."

"And when did this start?" I said.

"Monday," Brian said. Then his jaw dropped. Everyone in the band had the same startled expression. That was, of course, the same day the stink began. We finally had our answer.

"So you mean the Teen Fresh is what stinks?" Ross asked. We nodded. Ross looked skeptical. Slowly, reluctantly, he lifted up each one of his arms and stuck his nose in his own armpits. After one whiff, it looked like he was going to keel over.

"That's it, all right!" he said. "I can't believe it!"

For a second, I couldn't believe it either. How could they not know the smell was coming from them? I guess when you get enough people in a room, the smell just fills the air. Plus, it's kind of harder to tell when you're the one that smells bad. Especially since you don't want to believe it. After all, even here, with just four people, everyone thought it was coming from someone else. And then we found out what else threw them off.

"That's impossible!" said Jerome, sniffing himself again just to make sure he wasn't mistaken. From the look on his face, he wasn't. But he seemed *very* confused. "It's supposed to smell like vanilla!" he said desperately.

"That's right! It even smelled like vanilla when I put it on this morning!" Marisa added.

"Let's check that out!" PJ said. "Does anyone have any of that Teen Fresh stuff on them?"

"I do!" Marisa said. She reached down to the floor behind her drum kit and pulled a little deodorant roll-on out of a backpack. She tossed it over to PJ, who immediately uncapped and smelled it.

"It's vanilla, all right," PJ confirmed.

"But that's not what it smells like now, that's for sure," Brian said.

Something incredibly weird was going on. The Teen Fresh definitely started out as vanilla. But somehow, after a certain amount of time, it was turning nasty. The question was, how?

Keisha was scribbling furiously in her note pad, trying to get everything straight. "Okay, it seems like somehow, Snurdburg sabotaged this new deodorant. And it's on some kind of time delay. Until we find out more, you'd better lay off the Teen Fresh."

"Don't have to tell me twice," said Ross, as he packed up his keyboard equipment in a huff. "I'm throwing mine out as soon as I get home."

"As for us, Crew, we've got some more investigating to do," she said. "PJ, where does it say that stuff is made?"

PJ turned the Teen Fresh bottle around and squinted at the fine print on the back. "Oscar's Odors, Inc.," she read aloud. "Oscar de la Scenta, CEO."

"That must be that French guy we ran into yesterday!" Fernando said.

"Sounds like we need to pay him a visit, and fast," I said. "He's got to find out his Teen Fresh is being used for a nasty prank."

"Let's hit the tracks, Crew," Keisha said. "Brian, spread the word! Tell everyone to stop wearing that Teen Fresh stuff!"

"Sure thing," Brian said. "And then I'll start planning our revenge. Those Snurdheads have gone too far this time. They're gonna pay!"

I have to admit, I was a little worried about what that might mean. But we didn't have time to argue. We had to stop the Teen Fresh before it stunk again.

CHAPTER NINE

Get a Job

As soon as we figured out that the Teen Fresh deodorant was responsible for the stink at Peak Valley High, we hopped on the KC Express and took a ride out of town. Our mission: to find Oscar de la Scenta, president of the company that made Teen Fresh, and warn him that his product had been sabotaged. Once we stopped the smell at the source, maybe we could figure out just how those rotten Snurdburg kids managed to tamper with the deodorant in the first place.

Oscar's company, the Oscar's Odors Fragrance Factory, was about ten miles away, in an industrial park on the outskirts of . . . <u>Snurdburg</u>. Convenient, huh? I guess the Snurdburg kids didn't want to go too far out of their way.

I have to admit, though, that when we saw the factory up close, I wondered how they could have broken into it. It wasn't exactly user-friendly. It was basically a huge metal fortress with no windows. There was no front lobby, either—just a big heavy steel door at the top of some concrete steps, with a tiny intercom box on the wall next to it. We went up to the door, and I pushed the intercom button. A loud, annoying buzz greeted me back. Then a young man's voice came over the speaker . . .

"Oscar's Odors! All deliveries to the service entrance please! Thank you!" he said quickly. It sounded like he was about to hang up. Luckily PJ jumped in.

"Hold on!" she said. "We're not making a delivery!"

"You're not?" the man on the other end responded. He sounded surprised.

"No," PJ said. "We want to talk to Oscar de la Scenta, please!"

"Mr. de la Scenta is very busy," the man said. He sounded like he was going to hang up again.

"I think he'll want to talk to us," Keisha insisted. "We have some very disturbing information about his product."

"Yeah! He's got to take it off the market!" Fernando added.

There was a brief pause. Then the voice said, "Hold on, I'll put you through." After a couple of rings, a man with a French accent picked up. It was the voice of the man we had run into earlier.

"Oscar de la Scenta here!" he said. "What is it that you want?"

"It's the Kinetic City Super Crew," Keisha said.

"I have never heard of you," he replied.

"That doesn't matter," she said. "You've got to let us into your factory. We need to see how you're making the Teen Fresh."

Mr. de la Scenta sounded suspicious. "What do you mean, I have to let you into my factory?

117

No outsiders are allowed into my factory! My manufacturing techniques are top secret! And how do you know about Teen Fresh? That is only in the test marketing phase!"

"Yeah, and you've got to stop test marketing it! It stinks!" PJ said urgently.

That was the wrong thing to say. Mr. de la Scenta sounded mad. "What is this you are saying about my deodorant? How dare you come to my place of work and insult me!"

"No, you don't understand! It *really* stinks!" Fernando said, trying to explain. "It smells like rotten eggs!"

"Impossible!" the voice on the other end barked. "You obviously have never smelled my Teen Fresh masterpiece! Just what kind of a 'Snooping Crew' are you anyway? You must be corporate spies!"

"What?" I asked. This was getting way out of hand. "Spies for who?"

"Don't play dumb with me, you perfume-pirating pipsqueak!" Mr. de la Scenta snarled. The intercom crackled and hissed from the intensity of his voice. "You are working for Madame Fifi, my arch rival! She has been trying for years to steal my secrets for her own perfume company! And now she is using young people! For shame!"

"Hold everything," Fernando said. "You've got us all wrong. Don't you remember—we ran into you on your way out of Peak Valley High just yesterday . . ."

A gasp rattled through the speaker. "What! You mean you have been following me around too? How sneaky can you get? And to think I almost gave you some of my Teen Fresh right then and there! You go back to Madame Fifi and tell her I will never give my secrets to her pathetic French factory!"

It was a mistake, but I couldn't help asking. "Wait a minute—aren't *you* French?"

For a second, I wasn't sure if Mr. de la Scenta was going to faint or explode. He just huffed and puffed and finally let out a roar: "*French?* How dare you even insinuate that! I am *Belgian!* That's just like Madame Fifi—

and the French—to act like we do not even have our own country! *Mademoiselles* and *messieurs*, I have been insulted enough for one day! Goodbye!"

There was a loud click and then a harsh, droning dial tone on the other end of the intercom. We all looked at each other in defeat.

"Well, Crew, looks like we botched that one up," Keisha sighed.

"You can say that again," I said. "How do we find out what's happening to the Teen Fresh? We can't even get in the door here."

"We could try a battering ram," Fernando suggested jokingly.

"Actually, we may not need one," PJ said with a sly grin. She was staring over the railing at a service door on the side of the building. A bunch of workers were filing inside. Probably the late shift. "*They're* getting in, aren't they?" she asked. The tone of her voice suggested she had something clever up her sleeve.

"Yeah, but they *work* here," Keisha replied.

"And how do they know we don't?" PJ asked.

I knew where she was going with this, and I wasn't sure I liked it. "Come on, PJ," I said. "They're older. They'd know we're just high school kids."

"Actually, some of them look kind of young. I think you and Keisha could pass, at least," Fernando said, squinting at the workers in the distance.

"What about *you?*" I protested. "You're the same age as me!"

"Yeah, but I've got such boyish good looks," Fernando teased. "Besides, I need to keep PJ out of trouble." PJ hates when he says things like that. She gave him a swift punch in the arm. "See what I mean?" he said, laughing.

Keisha didn't look too excited about the idea, either. "I don't know," she said. "It seems like a sneaky thing to do."

"What choice do we have?" Fernando asked. "We tried talking to him. And besides, did it ever occur to you that Oscar de la Scenta is in on this scam?"

"Actually, it didn't," I said.

"Well, think again!" he replied. "Could a bunch of Snurdburg goons really break in here, mess with all his perfume equipment, and come out changing Teen Fresh in such a weird way? They don't know how to make deodorant. But somehow they managed not only to make it stink, but to actually fix it so it smells like vanilla at first, and then smells like rotten eggs later. Sounds like they had a little professional help," he said, knotting his fingers like he was narrating a detective story.

I thought about it. It seemed like it would be weird for Mr. de la Scenta to be involved. After all, it's his company, and Teen Fresh had his name right on every container. Why ruin his own reputation? Still, Fernando's point was worth considering.

Keisha seemed to agree. "Well, if we get in there, at the very least maybe we can figure out exactly how this Teen Fresh is made," she said. "That could help us figure out what's wrong with it, and maybe even catch whoever's messing with it red-handed."

"Not only that," PJ said, "but Curtis would get to see all their super-high-tech gear."

"That's right!" Fernando chimed in. "Think about it, Curtis. This is a state-of-the-art chemical plant. They've probably got equipment here like you've never seen before! Lots of great ideas for inventions . . ."

They sure knew how to press my buttons. Ever since we got Zorro, I *had* been thinking about making some chemical sensors of my own. This just might be the place to learn how. "Okay, fine," I said. "I guess I'll go in."

"That's the spirit," Fernando said. "While you and Keisha are in there, I'll go back to the train with PJ and do a few experiments. PJ, do you still have that Teen Fresh sample Marisa gave you?"

PJ reached into her jacket pocket. "Yup, here you go." She handed it to Fernando.

"What are we going to do with that?" PJ asked, backing away from it like it was some kind of a bomb.

"Everything we can think of," Fernando

explained. "At least until it starts to stink. Put it on, wipe it off, rub it, put it on cotton, put it on wool, and just let it sit. Then maybe we'll pin down exactly what makes this stuff go bad."

That made sense to me. Even though Fernando had given himself the easy job, I guess it was his idea and he had dibs. It looked like we had a plan.

"Just one thing," I said. "If it gets hairy in there, I can't promise we'll stick around. I'm not getting arrested for impersonating a perfume worker."

"Can you get arrested for that?" Keisha asked, raising her eyebrow.

"Don't worry, Curtis—if it gets too hot for you, just get out of the kitchen," Fernando said. "But let's give it our best shot. This may be our only chance to nail the bad guys and close this case. Are we in this?"

"We're in!" we all shouted, putting our hands together. Fernando and PJ dashed back to the KC Express, leaving Keisha and me to our new after-school jobs.

CHAPTER TEN

Undercover

It was hard to believe Keisha and I were about to sneak into a factory posing as employees. But it seemed like the only way to find out more about Teen Fresh. So I guess you can just call me Curtis the Corporate Spy. You know, it does have kind of a catchy ring to it. I just hoped I wouldn't be seeing it as a caption under my mug shot in the Kinetic City Gazette's police report.

Everything depended on not getting caught. The longer we could pass for employees, the more we could find out. We were dressed pretty much like the other workers, so at least that was a start. Looking like we knew what we were doing was going to be another story.

Fortunately, I had the Can-Do Communicator in my knapsack. It's a sort of two-way radio I rigged up so that we Crew members can talk to each other when we're separated. Fernando and PJ had another one back on the train, so we could always get in touch with them if things got hairy. And as soon as we stepped into the factory, that looked like a definite possibility . . .

"Wow!" Keisha said, keeping her voice down so she wouldn't attract attention. "When it comes to security, this place is no Peak Valley High School."

She wasn't kidding. The doors to the service entrance were made of six-inch-thick reinforced steel. To open them, you had to punch a code into a little numeric keypad on the wall. Fortunately, there was somebody right in front of us who knew what the code was, and we followed him in. As we stepped into the main part of the factory, a bunch of lights snapped at us—I couldn't tell if they were cameras or x-rays. I was afraid someone was going to stop us, but we made it inside without a hitch.

The place was enormous. There were all sorts of big metal tanks and pipes, all divided up by a network of long corridors, full of door-ways leading to who-knows-where. Just finding where they made Teen Fresh was going to be a challenge. *But one thing's for sure*, I thought. *In a place this big, it should be pretty easy not to get noticed . . .*

"Hey, you two!" a gruff voice bellowed from off to our right. I turned to see a burly man with big, bushy eyebrows and dark, beady eyes walking over to us. He moved quickly in his work boots and coveralls. *Oh great*, I thought to myself. *Fifteen seconds and already our cover's blown. I can't believe I let Fernando go back to the train . . .*

Meanwhile, Keisha held her ground. I could tell by the way her eyes were darting around that she was nervous. But her body stayed perfectly still, with her feet planted like concrete pillars on the floor beneath her. Mr. Eyebrows trotted up to us and stared us down.

"Are you Smith and Peterson?" he said, in some kind of New York accent. I glanced over at Keisha. I tried opening my mouth, but for some reason, words weren't coming out.

Fortunately, they came out of Keisha's mouth instead. "Yes, sir, we are," she said matter-of-factly.

The man nodded once. "You're late," he said. "You shouldn't be late. Oscar doesn't like it when you're late."

All I could do was shake my head and look sorry. "Um, yes sir. We know. I'm sure he doesn't."

Then his knotted eyebrows seemed to relax a little, and he cracked what might have been some kind of a smile. "Okay, then," he said. "First day, I'll give you a break. But next time, I'd better see some hustle."

Keisha and I both let out a little breath. We'd gotten past step one. "Sure thing, sir," Keisha replied, with more confidence than before.

"Okay, then," the guy replied. "My name's Frank. I'm your foreman. First rule: You got a problem, you come to me. Don't bother Oscar. Oscar doesn't like being bothered." Without missing a beat, he squinted at us a little. "You two look a little young to be working here," he said.

I couldn't tell if he was suspicious or just confused. But I said the first thing that came to my mind. "We skipped a couple grades," I blurted out.

Keisha gave me the quickest glare she could manage. But Frank seemed to buy it. He just shrugged and said, "Well, more power to ya. Come on, I'll show you what we do here, and then we'll get you started."

Score! I thought to myself. If anything was going to point us in the right direction, it was a factory tour for insiders. I nudged Keisha excitedly. She smiled, but tried not to react.

We took a left turn down the first big corridor. In between the big tanks, we could see into glass-walled labs with people working at all kinds of weird machines. "This here's our standard fragrance development center," Frank said. "Potpourri, rose petals, orange blossom. All that air freshener junk. Nothing fancy. But don't tell Oscar. Oscar likes to think all his perfumes are fancy."

"Oscar sounds like an interesting guy," I said, trying to make conversation.

"Yeah, but don't tell him that," Frank replied. "Oscar hates to be called interesting."

I wanted to ask if he also hates to be called 'suspicious,' but I thought that would get us booted.

"Now over there . . . *that's* where we do some interesting stuff," Frank said, pointing to a lab on our right. I saw a bunch of people sniffing little strips of paper, and then writing stuff down. "That's where they figure out what our different smells make people think of, or make them feel like doing. We got a contract with Lacy's Department Store to find a smell that makes people want to shop."

Keisha was shocked. "Are you serious? You actually do that?"

"Sure, it happens all over, kid," Frank replied. "You got a problem with it?"

"Well, it just seems a little sneaky," she said.

"Oh yeah?" Frank shot back. "What about when they pump that soft, lazy music in there that makes you feel like lollygagging around looking at stuff? What about when they do up all those nice window displays to lure you in? Everything in a store's designed to make you want to spend money there. Why not the smell, too?"

I guess he had a point. Keisha didn't argue with him. I wasn't sure if that was because she agreed, or if she was just trying to avoid trouble.

We rounded a corner and passed by another glass-enclosed lab. In this one, everyone was wearing little white cloth face masks, like the kind doctors wear. "What's in there?" I asked.

"Oh, that's the B.O. lab," Frank replied casually.

"*B.O.* lab?" Keisha asked.

"Yeah, that's what I said. You got a problem with it?" Frank shot back.

"No, of course not," I jumped in. "But doesn't B.O. stand for body odor?"

"Sure does. One of our worst enemies. Although it doesn't really come *from* your body. It comes from bacteria that live *on* your body."

"Gross!" Keisha said.

"It's true," Frank replied. "The little buggers live on your skin and eat some of the chemicals in your sweat. The chemicals themselves don't smell bad, but once the bacteria eat them and pass their gas, bang! It's time to hit the showers."

Ugh. The thought of bacteria living in my armpits and eating my sweat was too disgusting to think about. Even though I know all kinds of bacteria live inside and outside us, and a lot of them are even good for you, it's not an idea that's easy to get used to.

"So what exactly do you *do* in the B.O. lab?" Keisha asked. Now she sounded interested.

"Well, it's like this, see," Frank explained. "We're trying to find another chemical that those bacteria like to eat, but that won't make them crank out the smelly stuff," Frank explained. "If we can do that, and make it into an underarm deodorant, we can stop B.O. before it starts."

"Hey, speaking of underarm deodorants," I said, "where do they make the Teen Fresh?"

Frank's eyes narrowed. "How'd you hear of that?"

Keisha thought fast. "My little brother goes to Peak Valley High," she said.

It was a good save. Frank seemed to relax again. "Oh. Well, then you probably know that's in a secret development phase. We gotta be careful about spies and all. The only way you're gonna get in on that project is to talk to Chief Snidely."

The sound of that name almost stopped me in my tracks. "Chief *Snidely?*" I asked. "That wouldn't be the old principal of Peak Valley, would it?"

"As a matter of fact, yeah," Frank said. "She's in charge of the whole Teen Fresh project. And she must really like that school. She insisted that they be the ones to get the free samples. I hear she really twisted Oscar's arm about it. And believe me, Oscar doesn't like to have his arm twisted."

My head was spinning. A really nasty ex-principal pushing bad Teen Fresh at her old school? While she has access to all the machinery? Suddenly a faceless Snurdburg delinquent didn't seem like our number one suspect anymore.

"Tell you what. If you two really want to work on Teen Fresh, I'll start you off in the mercaptan unit. The Teen Fresh lab's right next door. You can try to get a word in with Snidely on your break. I gotta warn you, though: make sure it's a big word. Zelda's really into her vocabulary."

"Hold on," Keisha said. "Did you say the *mercaptan* unit was right next door to the Teen Fresh lab?"

"Yeah," Frank said, looking confused. "You know, the mercaptans. For the gas company. We make those here too. They don't smell pretty, but they're some of our best moneymakers . . ."

Just then I heard a low buzz. It was coming from my knapsack. The Can-Do Communicator! What were Fernando and PJ calling *us* for? Didn't they know we were trying to *avoid* attention?

I wished they would hang up, but they didn't. Frank was looking around, trying to figure out where the sound was coming from. "Either of you have a beeper or a cell phone?" he said.

It was my turn to think on my feet. I wish I had Keisha's knack for it. "Um, that's . . . er, my timer," I explained fitfully. "I've got to take my anti-nausea medication. I've got this disease . . ."

"What disease?" Frank asked curiously.

"Barfulitis," I replied. It was the best I could do off the top of my head. I grabbed my stomach like I was going to hurl. "Will you excuse me for a minute?"

Frank nodded. He looked a little suspicious, but he also looked like he wanted me as far away as possible. "Okay, okay," he said. "Go on around the corner. Room 121 is empty." We thanked him quickly and jogged around to the empty room, shutting the door behind us.

"Good one, Captain Barfulitis," Keisha said, snickering.

"Hey, it worked, didn't it?" I replied. I fished the Can-Do Communicator out of my knapsack and hit the "talk" button. "Curtis here!" I whispered loudly into the speaker.

"Curtis! It's Nando! We found out what makes the Teen Fresh stink!"

"That's great, but why did you have to call us?" Keisha hissed. "We were talking to one of the foremen here! You could have blown our cover."

Fernando hesitated for just a second. "Whoops," he said. "Sorry about that. But listen—PJ and I figured it out! It's the heat!"

"Heat?" I said.

"Yeah! We tried everything, and for a while nothing was making the Teen Fresh stink. PJ and I were even wearing it. It still smelled like vanilla. But then I tried heating it up."

"He almost set the Kitchen Car on fire!" PJ yelled from the background.

"Shhh!" Fernando tried to quiet PJ down, but it was too late. "We had a little trouble with the stove," he explained. "No big deal. But boy, you warm that stuff up and it stinks to high heaven!"

"You know, that actually makes sense," Keisha said.

"How?" I asked.

"Think about it, Curtis. The smell always seemed to kick in whenever people were doing something important. Something stressful. And what happens when you get all worked up and stressed out?"

"You sweat?" I answered.

On the other end of the communicator, Fernando clicked into Keisha's train of thought.

"Yeah, and your body heats up! Of course! That explains a lot!" He was right. It did make sense.

"Well, check this out. We've found out a few things ourselves," Keisha said. I could feel the excitement starting to build. The pieces were falling into place.

"Like what?" Fernando asked.

"Like Ex-Principal Snidely from Peak Valley runs the Teen Fresh lab!" I said.

"And it's right next to the mercaptans!" Keisha added.

"Whoa! Did somebody say, 'new suspect?'" Fernando asked.

"Our thoughts exactly," I said. "Snidely's got the know-how and the access to mess with the Teen Fresh. And she's nasty."

"But what's her motive?" Keisha asked.

"Maybe she wants to get even with Peak Valley for something," Fernando suggested. "Let's face it, she wasn't exactly well-liked over there."

"Good point, Nando," I said. "And now that we know when the Teen Fresh smells bad, we just have to figure out how it's made. Then we'll blow the lid off this thing once and for all!"

"Oh you will, will you?" a voice snapped from behind us. A chill went up my spine. I turned around. It was Frank. He'd come in through another door we hadn't even noticed.

"Barfulitis, my foot," he said accusingly. "I should have known you two were spies! Working for Madame Fifi, I bet!"

"No, really," Keisha protested. "You've got it all wrong!"

"I think I had it all wrong when I trusted you! Oscar doesn't like spies, you know! And neither does Frank!" He lunged toward us.

That's when instinct took over. "Run, Keisha!" I shouted. We both took off like lightning. Keisha peeled ahead of me with her track-team sprint. I managed to keep up somehow. Luckily the boots and coveralls slowed Frank down. We tore down the long corridors, back to the door we came in, and burst out into the open air.

As we ran toward the KC Express, we passed a guy and a girl, a little older than us, who were heading toward the factory. "Hey!" the girl said. "Do you know where we can find a guy named Frank in there? We're starting work with him today!"

"Are you Smith and Peterson?" I asked them.

"Yeah," the guy said. "How'd you know?"

"You're late!" I answered. Before they had time to say anything else, we had disappeared out of sight.

CHAPTER ELEVEN

The Principal Issues

After escaping the clutches of Frank, the bushy-eyebrowed foreman at the smell factory, we met Fernando and PJ back in the Control Car to go over the facts. We knew that Ex-Principal Snidely could have sabotaged the Teen Fresh if she wanted to. And based on what we saw and what the other kids had told us about her, she sure could be nasty enough to do it.

The question was, did she have a reason? We never did find out why she stopped being principal at Peak Valley. If she got fired, that would be a perfect motive for revenge. But we wanted to make sure. So the next

day, we paid Principal Marsh another visit.
Maybe if he understood what we knew already,
he'd tell us more about what happened to Ms.
Snidely.

His office was back to its old self. There
were more aromatherapy candles than ever, and
the whole place smelled like flowers and spice.
Weird, spacey mood music was coming from some
speakers on his top bookshelf. As he ushered
us in, he turned down the music, sat cross-
legged on the floor and offered us seats on
some fancy cushions along his wall . . .

"So, how's your investigation going? It seems
like you've made some progress," Principal
Marsh said. "Today's math exam was surpris-
ingly odor-free."

"Well, yeah, we found out a lot of things,"
Keisha replied. "First off, we know the Teen
Fresh is causing it."

"That deodorant they've been giving out?"
the principal asked. "But I thought it smelled
like vanilla."

"That's the problem," Fernando explained. "It smells like vanilla at first. But when you've had it on a while, and it heats up, it starts to reek."

"That's why the students smelled it in all those high-stress situations," Keisha explained. "Their bodies were heating up, and that activated the stink part of the Teen Fresh."

"Well, I'll be!" Principal Marsh said. "That sure is fascinating. How does that work?"

"That's what we don't know," PJ said. "But we think we found out who might."

"Who?" the principal asked.

"Ex-Principal Snidely," she replied. "She works on Teen Fresh at the factory. And they make smelly mercaptans right next door to her lab."

Principal Marsh's face fell a little bit. "I see," he said. He looked kind of disturbed.

Now was the time to ask. "Principal Marsh?" I said delicately. "Is there any reason Ms. Snidely would want to make Peak Valley High School look bad?"

"Or smell bad?" Fernando added.

Principal Marsh sighed, and hung his head in his knees for a second. Then he looked up. "Well, I had hoped it wouldn't come to this, but I guess Zelda's coping strategies aren't what I hoped they were." He pushed his glasses up nervously. "As you probably guessed, Zelda was separated from the Peak Valley community on . . . less than friendly terms."

"I knew it!" Keisha exclaimed. She took out her notebook and started scribbling furiously. "What happened?"

"Well, frankly, it was her treatment of the students that did her in," Principal Marsh said. "You saw how harsh she is with them. Well, that's nothing compared to when she actually ran the school. Once, she actually had some of her friends in the police department arrest a freshman for chewing gum, just to make an example of him! Can you imagine?"

We all gasped. That beat a lot of stories about teachers that were just made up. "That's pretty harsh," Keisha said. She could be a master of understatement.

"That kind of thing went on all the time," Principal Marsh went on. "Bad grammar and spelling were the worst offenses. One mistake on a test or a paper, and it was a week's worth of after-school work."

"Well, that's a lot, but at least it's a little more normal," I said.

"It was a week's worth of work at *her house!* She'd make the kids weed her garden, shovel her driveway, and rearrange her dining room furniture. She even made a bunch of sophomores put in a new roof! And I don't want to tell you what happened to the kids who had to clean out her furnace."

"Oh," I said. "I guess that's a little out of line."

"You're telling me!" Principal Marsh sighed. "It all came to a head when we were having a faculty meeting about . . . her future at the school."

"You mean when you were talking about firing her?" Fernando said bluntly.

"Exactly. We were all unhappy with the way she'd been acting, but I just got so worked up about the effect on the students' mental health that I, well, lost it."

"Oh no! Did you get into a fight?" PJ asked.

"Not exactly," he replied. "I just told her flat out: 'Zelda, I've seen the way you treat these kids and it *stinks!*' Everyone cheered. That was pretty much the clincher—we voted her out right after that."

"I guess she didn't take it too well," Keisha said.

"Oh, she was furious. Vowed to get her revenge on me and the school and everything I hold dear. Make my life stink instead of hers. That sort of thing. I've been trying to give her the benefit of the doubt, but I guess maybe she's let her little inner meanies get the best of her."

"Well, Crew, I think the evidence against Ms. Snidely is pretty hard," PJ said.

"It's still circumstantial, though," I pointed out. "We still need to prove she deliberately botched up the Teen Fresh."

"Well, even so, it's a good thing we heard this story," Fernando said. He turned to Mr. Marsh. "See, all this time we thought it was Snurdburg kids playing another prank," he explained.

"Oh, is that what your friend Brian was talking about?" Principal Marsh replied.

Something about his tone made me worry. "What? When?" I asked.

"I just overheard him talking to his friends from the basketball team. They said they were going to get even with Snurdburg once and for all. I thought they were just talking about beating them in the game. But I didn't know what sneaking into Snurdburg's locker room had to do with that."

"Uh-oh," PJ said. "It sounds like some kind of revenge plot! Mr. Marsh, why didn't you stop them?"

Principal Marsh looked embarrassed. "I didn't want to interrupt," he said meekly. "They were talking about meeting in the cafeteria in a few minutes." He glanced down at his watch.

"I'll bet they're still there now. You might be able to catch them."

"We'd better," Keisha said. We bolted out the door. If you'd asked me a couple days earlier, I never would have thought we'd end up trying to save *Snurdburg* from a prank. Now, that was exactly what we had to do.

CHAPTER TWELVE

Talking Trash

When we last left Brian and his friends, we kind of left them with something dangerous: a taste for revenge on Snurdburg. I had figured it was all talk--after all, if there's one thing Brian's good at, it's talk. But judging from what Principal Marsh told us he overheard, it sounded like Snurdburg was in for a payback that they didn't deserve.

We rushed straight down to the cafeteria, hoping to catch them before they did anything really nasty. I hoped we weren't too late. The last thing we needed was for the Super Crew to be responsible for some kind of prank war. When we first opened the cafeteria doors, though, it looked like they were gone. The whole lunchroom was deserted. There was only one sign of life . . .

"Ugh!" PJ said, as soon as she took a step inside the lunchroom. "Do you smell that?"

I sure did. Believe me, the only way you could miss it is if you had a world-class cold or a bargain-basement nose job. It was one of the grossest things that's ever gone in or out of my nostrils, if you get my drift. It made the rotten egg Teen Fresh smell like a rose garden.

"It's worse than that dead squirrel in our chimney!" Keisha said, holding her nose.

"Where the heck is it coming from?" Fernando asked.

I stepped around the room. The closer I got to the kitchen, the worse it got. "I think it's in there!" I said, pointing to the kitchen door. Then suddenly, a loud whirring sound, like from a blender or some kind of machine, came from behind the door.

"Someone's in there!" Keisha said.

"Maybe it's them! Let's go in!" said PJ.

We walked slowly up to the kitchen door— we kind of had to get used to the smell bit by bit. Finally, we knocked. "Brian? You in there?" I yelled. No answer. The machine noise had to be drowning me out anyway. I signaled to the rest of the Crew to follow me, and swung the door open.

There he was, all right. I saw Brian, all of his band mates, his friend Chad from the basketball team, a couple other guys in basketball jerseys, and even that girl Gwen from the debate team. They were standing around an industrial-size mixing bowl, blending together a disgusting green sludge in the electric mixer. The counters were covered with buckets full of some unrecognizable glop. And the smell was ten times worse.

Brian noticed us and shut off the mixer. The whirring noise stopped. "Hey, Curtis, you're just in time," Brian said. "We're throwing together a little thank-you gift for Snurdburg."

"Yeah—for that special Teen Fresh!" Marisa the drummer sneered. She scraped a brown, moldy goo out of one of the buckets and dumped it into the mixing bowl. She coughed and hacked a little when the smell hit her.

I was about to tell them that Snurdburg probably wasn't to blame, but PJ cut me off before I even opened my mouth.

"What the heck is all this stuff?" she asked. "And this awful smell?"

"You like it?" asked Chad, the basketball player. "We figured, since Snurdburg's into smells, we'd give them a taste of their own medicine. So we thought, where's the worst smelling stuff we can find?"

"So we went to the dumpster behind the cafeteria. It doesn't get any worse than that," said Ross, the red-headed keyboard player. "This stuff didn't smell too good when it was fresh—and it's been rotting in the trash for days!"

"Hold on," Keisha said. "Snurdburg may not actually deserve this . . ."

"You mean it's too good for 'em?" Gwen interrupted. "We know what you mean. That's why we dug deep and weren't afraid to let it get ugly." She held up a big wooden spoon with some goop stuck to it, which looked kind of like macaroni and cheese, except it was greenish-gray. Keisha doesn't get spooked easily, but she backed away from the stuff on Gwen's spoon like it was going to spring to life any second.

"I can't wait to go to Snurdburg and spread this crud around! That'll teach them to mess with Peak Valley!" yelled Jerome, the Bucket guitar player, from the back of the kitchen.

"YEAH!" his teammates cheered in reply.

"Hold on!" I said. "Snurdburg probably didn't mess up the Teen Fresh! That's what we've been trying to tell you."

Everyone turned to me, looking confused. "What do you mean? They've been after us for years!" Ross said.

"Maybe, but we don't think they're behind this," Keisha said. "All the evidence points to your ex-principal, Ms. Snidely!"

"She works at the Teen Fresh factory. And she wants to get her revenge on Peak Valley!" PJ added.

Everyone turned to each other and started chattering excitedly. Then Brian spoke up. "Are you all sure? I mean, I've heard Snidely was bad, but I don't think she'd pull a stunt like this."

"Oh, yes she would," said Jerome. "I wouldn't put anything past her. One time I was late for class, and she made me clean out her car engine with a toothbrush. While it was still running!" The other, more experienced Peak Valley students voiced their agreement.

"So, please, can you hold off on your revenge stunt?" Keisha pleaded. "We've almost got this case solved."

There was silence for a couple seconds. Then Brian spoke up. "Well, I guess it *was* a pretty stupid thing to do," he admitted with a sigh.

"Wait—did you mean 'stoopid?' As in cool?" Chad asked.

"No, just as in dumb," Brian replied. "Even if Snurdburg was doing it, why sink to their level? Let's just beat them fair and square all weekend long," he replied. "Besides," he said, gesturing toward a couple buckets of moldy tuna fish, "this stuff reeks!"

"Well, I'm glad we stopped that disaster," Keisha said. "Now we've got to get back to the Oscar's Odors factory. We've still got to prove beyond a doubt that Ms. Snidely's responsible, and stop her once and for all."

"Oh, no, not the factory again!" I moaned. "I can think of a lot of things I'd rather do than go back to *that* place."

Meanwhile Brian and his friends were staring with dread at the mess they'd made. "Well, Curtis," PJ said, "you *could* stay here and help these guys clean up . . ."

That changed my mind real quick. "The factory it is!" I said. "Come on, Crew, let's get back to the train!"

CHAPTER THIRTEEN

A Little Grain of Truth

After we stopped the Peak Valley kids from stink-attacking Snurdburg's High School, we hopped back on the KC Express and went straight back to the Oscar's Odors factory. We weren't expecting Oscar de la Scenta to be happy to see us, but at least now we had more facts to persuade him with. Of course, that's assuming he wasn't in on the scam himself. If he was, we were in for a really rough time.

We walked up to the big, heavy main door, and Keisha hit the intercom buzzer. The same male voice that answered on our last visit picked up . . .

"Oscar's Odors! No visitors allowed!" the voice snapped. "Have a nice day!"

"Wait!" PJ said. "We have to talk to Oscar de la Scenta!"

"Oscar's very busy. Who's this?" the voice answered.

All of a sudden Keisha jumped in with her best French accent. "It is Madame Fifi, you fool! My business is down in the dumps! I have come to offer Oscar a truce! Perhaps see if he would like to buy my company, even! Unless he would like me to take my offer elsewhere."

There was a brief silence. Then the voice on the other end stammered: "Yes ma'am, Madame Fifi, I'll . . . send him right out!" The intercom clicked off.

"Well, I hope *that* worked," I said.

"All we have to do is get him to talk to us," Keisha assured me. "Then the evidence will speak for itself."

"Unless he's in cahoots with Ms. Snidely. Then he'll probably kidnap us and let us rot in some kind of smelly torture chamber!" Fernando said dramatically.

"Yeah, I guess that's another possibility," I sighed. Fernando had taken that straight from the plot of *The Dungeon of a Thousand Dentists*, another one of his favorite sci-fi flicks.

Suddenly the big steel door burst open, and Mr. de la Scenta himself stepped out. It was definitely the same guy we ran into that day at Peak Valley High. I'd recognize that mustache anywhere.

"What is this?" Mr. de la Scenta exclaimed when he saw us standing there. He looked confused and disturbed. "None of you are Madame Fifi! Especially him!" he said, pointing to me for some reason.

"No, it's us," Keisha explained. "The Kinetic City Super Crew!"

"We really need to talk to you about Teen Fresh. And Ms. Snidely," Fernando added quickly.

"*Mon dieu!*" Oscar exclaimed. He threw his hands in the air angrily and let out a disgusted snort through his thick mustache. "Of all the rotten dirty tricks! Will you little spies never leave me alone?"

"Look, Mr. de la Scenta," I said firmly. "We're not spies. Just hear us out. That Snidely character you've got working for you is bad news!"

"Nonsense!" he replied. "She is a model employee!"

"Oh, yeah?" I said. "Well, we think your model employee is ruining your Teen Fresh!"

"That's right," Fernando added. "It smells like rotten eggs when you heat it! A little strange for a deodorant, don't you think? Unless you made it smell like that on purpose . . ."

Mr. de la Scenta raised an eyebrow and stopped thoughtfully for a second. But then he waved his hand dismissively. "This is ridiculous! I do not believe you! My Teen Fresh would never smell in such an awful way!"

"Okay, if you really don't believe us, smell it for yourself," Keisha said. She pulled Marisa's Teen Fresh from her pocket, and rolled some of it on her palms. Then she held them up to Mr. de la Scenta's nose. He took a whiff.

"Yes, so? It is my natural vanilla fragrance. The top of the line," he replied.

"Okay, now wait just a second," Keisha said. She rubbed her hands together hard and fast for a minute or so. As she did it, I began to smell something familiar. When she stuck her palms up at Mr. de la Scenta's nose again, he almost fell over from shock.

"*Now* what does it smell like?" Keisha said.

"Ugh! *Mercaptans!* It cannot be!" Oscar cried. "But I have smelled them with my own nose! They must be in the microcapsules!"

"Micro-whatsles?" PJ asked.

"Oh dear!" Oscar said. He looked around nervously, as if to see if anyone else had heard him. "I have spilled the beans! I never once have mentioned the secrets of Teen Fresh to an outsider! My silence is broken!"

He took a deep breath and rubbed his temples. He looked really upset. If he had anything to do with this stink, he sure was doing a great acting job. "I suppose I have no choice. This Teen Fresh is a disgrace to my name. Perhaps Ms. Snidely *has* done something terrible. I suppose we must share our information with each other."

"That would be nice," I said, trying not to sound too pushy.

"Come in," Oscar said, ushering us through the doorway. "We will go someplace where we cannot be heard."

He led us to a set of elevators just inside the main door. There was a keypad next to them that looked like a push-button phone. Mr. de la Scenta punched in about nine or ten numbers, and an elevator arrived with a *DING!* We rode it up to the top floor. Then he led us to what looked like part of a wall.

"Step into my office," he said.

"Sure thing," Fernando replied, smiling nervously. "Where's the door?"

Mr. de la Scenta reached into his pocket and pulled out something that looked like a pocket calculator. He punched in a few more numbers, and suddenly one panel of the wall we were staring at opened up. It was a built-in secret door! I promised myself to ask him where he got that. It would be awesome to install one in the KC Express.

We sat down in his office and told him the whole story about what had been going on with the Teen Fresh at Peak Valley. He looked absolutely heartbroken. This was a guy who took pride in his smells, and the fact that everyone knew Teen Fresh stunk really got to him.

Then we told him all about Ex-Principal Snidely, and all the mean stuff she used to do, and how she wanted revenge on Peak Valley for losing her job. Again, he seemed surprised and upset. Ms. Snidely never told him she got fired from her old job. But he had to believe our side of the story. There didn't seem to be any other explanation for what was going on. Ms. Snidely was the only one who had access to the Teen Fresh machinery, besides Mr. de la Scenta himself.

"Now I know why she insisted on marketing Teen Fresh at Peak Valley High," he said with a sigh. "She told me she wanted to give something back to her old school. Little did I know she meant a stinky rotten egg smell!"

"Yeah, it's been pretty bad over there," Keisha said. "And that rotten egg smell kicks in at the worst possible time—whenever the students get stressed out."

Mr. de la Scenta winced. "Oh, those words are like little arrows through my Belgian perfume-making heart!" he whimpered. "Because that is the exact opposite of what the Teen Fresh was meant to do."

This was the part we still didn't understand, so I pressed him on. "Yeah—what *was* it supposed to do?" I asked. "Does it have something to do with those microcapsules you mentioned?"

"Ah yes," he replied. "It has everything to do with them." He opened his desk drawer and ripped out some drawings. One showed a bunch of little round beads with a tiny bluish cloud inside of each one.

"Behold, the secret to Teen Fresh. Microcapsules. They are little tiny hollow beads, so small you cannot even see them. They are specially designed to melt under just the right amount of body heat. And each one is filled with my vanilla-scented fragrance."

"I thought that was just soaked into the deodorant," Keisha said.

"Oh, it is!" Oscar replied. "You have your normal vanilla perfume when you put it on, just like in any other deodorant. But suppose later in the day, after the smell starts to wear off, you face a stressful situation. You are feeling a little hot and a little sweaty and perhaps a little stinky, no?"

"I guess so," Fernando said.

"Well, that's where the microcapsules come in! Once your body gets hot enough, the capsules melt, the extra perfume is released and—*poof!*—you have an extra burst of vanilla-scented deodorant protection!"

"Or, in this case, rotten egg-scented," I pointed out.

"Precisely," Mr. de la Scenta sighed. "It looks like Ms. Snidely has put the mercaptans in the microcapsules." He looked sad, but after thinking for a second, his eyes lit up. "But maybe there is hope! Maybe she did not do it to be mean! The mercaptan tank is located right next door! It could have been a mistake!"

I shrugged. "I guess it's possible," I said. "The only way to know for sure is to see for ourselves."

"You're right! And I know exactly how," Oscar replied. "Curtis—do you think you can pretend to work here?" he asked.

Not again! I thought. I opened my mouth to speak, but Keisha cut me off.

"Oh, sure," Keisha said. "He's a natural actor!"

"I don't know," I said, trying to back out. "I think we're all pretty good at undercover work."

"Well, then I guess I'd like the person who's most comfortable with technology," Oscar said. "After all, my smell factory is state of the art! If you are going to pass as one of my employees, you'll need lots of mechanical expertise."

"Then you picked the right guy. Curtis the Can-Man is the one for you," PJ said. "He knows technology inside and out."

"I can't think of anyone better for the job," Fernando added with a smirk.

"Then it is settled," Oscar said, shaking my hand. "You shall be Ms. Snidely's first personal assistant!"

I wanted to say something, but words just didn't come to me. Somehow my big mouth had decided not to open anymore. Too bad that happened one sentence too late.

CHAPTER FOURTEEN

Showdown at the Scent Shop

Well, somehow I had gotten myself roped into impersonating an Oscar's Odors worker again. This time, though, my boss was going to be Ex-Principal Snidely herself. Too bad I didn't have a chance to brush up on my grammar and vocabulary.

The plan was pretty simple. Oscar would tell Ms. Snidely that I was her new personal assistant. Because she'd seen us all before, I had to wear a disguise. I had a paste-on mustache, which itched like crazy, and a pair of glasses, which kept sliding down my nose.

Anyway, since I was supposed to be the new guy on the block, she'd have to show me how she made—or sabotaged—the Teen Fresh. Meanwhile, Oscar and the rest of the Crew would be listening in from the next room, through the Can-Do Communicator. As soon as she confessed, they'd spring in and surprise her.

If I had the chance to pick, I think I would have stayed behind the scenes. But hey, a Super Crew member never backs down from a challenge. At least that's what everyone keeps telling me. So I went with Oscar to the Teen Fresh lab, mustache and all, with the Can-Do Communicator hidden inside my jacket. I also had a gas mask in my knapsack, just in case . . .

"Zelda?" Oscar said, knocking lightly on the door as we peeked into the lab. Ms. Snidely flipped back her frizzy hair to reveal her famous scowl. She didn't look excited to see a stranger in her lab.

I set my knapsack down by my feet and looked around. It was a pretty big room. There were a whole lot of tanks, pumps, and

170

machines over by the far wall, near a back door. From a technical point of view, the equipment didn't look too hard to figure out, but I sure wished I had more time.

Meanwhile, Ms. Snidely tried to put her best face on. "Hello, Oscar," she said, as sweetly as she could manage. "Who's this with you?"

Oscar patted me on the back and gave me a little shove in Zelda's direction. "Say *bonjour* to Elmo," he said. *Elmo? He couldn't think of a better name?* I thought. "Your new personal assistant," Oscar explained.

Ms. Snidely raised an eyebrow. "Why, Oscar, what a nice gesture," she said through a tight, fake smile. "But I don't think I need an assistant. I'm quite content in my little monocracy."

"Monocracy?" Oscar asked.

"Literally, a government run by one person," Ms. Snidely explained quickly. "Or in this case, a deodorant lab run by one person." She forced a little giggle.

"Ah, but I think you do," Oscar insisted. "We're going to step up the Teen Fresh campaign at Peak Valley. I want to send them a whole new batch to help them smell nice in their difficult times. I think I'll even give some to the teachers, too." Ms. Snidely's eyes lit up with attention. Oscar took a step in and continued his sales pitch. "Think about it, Zelda. Maybe we'll try a new slogan: Teen Fresh—it is not just for teens anymore!"

I could almost see the wheels turning in Ms. Snidely's head. Finally, she said the magic words. "Very well, Oscar. I'll train Elmo here to help with the Teen Fresh. Perhaps he can do the busywork and give me time to pursue matters more noetic!"

"Noetic?" Oscar asked, looking baffled.

Ms. Snidely rolled her eyes. "Intellectual. Brainy," she replied. "Like new slogans and marketing plans. I want this deodorant to change Peak Valley High School forever!" she said, just a little menacingly.

"I like your enthusiasm, Zelda," Oscar

replied, winking at me. "Well, I'll leave you two to your work. I must go back to my office. Very far from this room. Good luck, Elmo!" he said to me, and shut the door behind them.

Up until now, I hadn't said a word. To be honest, I didn't really know what to do next. It must have showed.

"Well, don't just stand there looking exanimate!"

"Ex—what?" I asked. Between Ms. Snidely and Brian, this case was making me feel like I was in a foreign country.

"EXANIMATE!" Ms. Snidely snapped. "Lifeless or appearing lifeless!" With Oscar gone, she sure went back to her usual self in a hurry. "Let's get those gas machines cranking, Elmo! We've got some Teen Fresh to make!"

She stood back and waited for me to do something. What it was, I had no idea. She definitely didn't realize she was dealing with a beginner. I picked up my knapsack—just in case—and walked over to the machinery against the far wall. For a minute I just stared at them, desperately trying to figure out where the "on" switch was.

"Oh, for heaven's sake!" Ms. Snidely yelled. "What kind of a moron are you? Just flip the switch marked "VANILLA" on the left-hand side!"

Suddenly I realized that acting dumb just might work to my advantage. The more I could get her to say out loud, the better. I leaned over the machinery to block her view, and as carefully as I could, I reached into my jacket and flipped on the Can-Do Communicator. She didn't notice. Now every word was being sent directly to Oscar and the Crew.

Then I found the VANILLA switch, connected to a long black tube that went into some other machine, and put my finger on it.

"This VANILLA switch?" I said.

"Yes!" Ms. Snidely replied.

"What for?" I asked.

"To put the smell in the microcapsules, you ninny," she shot back.

Vanilla in the microcapsules? I thought. *Could she really be making a mistake?* My eyes darted quickly around the machinery. Then I noticed something that definitely looked wrong. The tube connected to the VANILLA switch actually had a second tube stuck in it. And that one didn't look like part of the machine—it was a different color and a different size, and was patched on with duct tape. To top it off, when I followed its path with my eyes, I noticed the extra tube led right into a hole in the back wall. From what I remembered, that was the wall that connected to the mercaptan lab.

I turned to Ms. Snidely and called to her as loudly as I could. "Hey, boss, there's some extra tube stuck in this machine. It looks like it's connected to the other room. I'm gonna pull it out now." I made a big show of tugging at the tube.

Ms. Snidely reacted instantly. "No, you idiot!" she shouted. "What are you doing? That tube is hooked up there for a reason!"

"It doesn't look right," I said, and with a yank, the extra tube came out. When it did, I heard a loud hissing sound, and the now-familiar smell of mercaptans hit my nose.

"No! The mercaptans!" Ms. Snidely cried. I turned toward her so the hidden Can-Do Communicator could pick her up loud and clear. "You don't understand, Elmo, but they have to go into the Teen Fresh! Just trust me and stop being so obdurate!" She didn't even wait for me to ask. "That means stubbornly persistent in wrongdoing!"

Bull's eye! I thought. She had pretty much admitted she was putting the mercaptans in on purpose. *Just a little more confession time for good measure,* I figured, *and then I'll call in the Crew.* In the meantime, that rotten egg smell was really getting to me. I reached into my knapsack and pulled out my trusty gas mask. But I barely had it on my head for one breath before Ms. Snidely ripped it right off my head!

"What's going on here?" she screamed, clutching the mask tightly in her arms. She reached over with one hand and ripped off my fake mustache. *Ow!* It was like having an industrial-strength Band-Aid torn off my face. "I should have known! That disguise had me going for a minute, but I'd recognize that ridiculous mask anywhere!"

Uh-oh. The mask! She'd seen it when we first met her at Peak Valley! Keisha was right. I should never have worn it in public.

"Who are you and why are you following me?" Ms. Snidely growled.

"I'm from the Kinetic City Super Crew," I said in my best Tough Cop voice, "and you're busted."

"You just stay out of my business!" Ms. Snidely snapped. "This is between me and Peak Valley! You'll never stop me from getting my revenge!" With that, she ran out the back door with my gas mask. I pulled out the Communicator.

"Crew! Get in here!" I said. "Our suspect's getting away!" In a flash, Oscar, Fernando, PJ, and Keisha burst in through the other door.

PJ had a backpack slung over her shoulder. I didn't know what she could possibly need to carry with her at a time like this, but there was no time to bring it up.

"She went that way!" I said, pointing toward the other door. "Come on!" We all tore out of the room and into a long corridor.

"We heard every word!" Oscar said, as we ran. "The scoundrel! Nobody soils the name of Oscar de la Scenta!"

"We'd just better find her before she escapes!" Fernando said.

As we came to a four-way intersection in the corridors, I heard a door swing open around the corner to the left. We got to the crossroads just in time to see a door down the hall slam shut.

"That must be her!" I said.

"Drat!" Oscar panted, trying to catch his breath. "She has gone into the B.O. lab!"

Uh-oh, I thought. I remembered the B.O. lab from that afternoon with Frank. It sounded like the nastiest place in the whole factory. Who knew what we would have to face up to in there? And there I was without my gas mask!

PJ wasn't concerned, though. "B.O. or no B.O., we're going in!" she said firmly.

We followed PJ to the nearest door to the lab. But just as we got near it, a figure emerged from another door at the far end. It was Ms. Snidely—and she was wearing *my* gas mask! Not only that, she had a couple of metal tanks strapped to her back. The tanks were attached to a pair of hoses that she was brandishing like pistols. It looked like something out of Fernando's bad sci-fi movies.

"Don't take another step! I'm armed!" she shouted through the mask.

"Armed with what?" PJ said.

"With stink power!" she said menacingly. "An extract from the gas of sweat-eating bacteria! Known to the uneducated as body odor. And in this concentrated form, baby, it makes a football locker room smell like a lilac garden," she said, grinning mischievously.

PJ tried to rush her anyway, but Oscar held her back. "Stand back, everyone!" he said. "Those are industrial-strength spray jets! If you get too close, the pressure alone could knock you on your back!"

"Not to mention the smell," Ms. Snidely sneered.

"You'll never get away with this, Snidely!" PJ shouted.

"On the contrary, my impish one," she replied, "that's precisely what I plan to do. I'm going right down this hall, out the door, and straight out of town. And don't try to follow me, or I'll blow you away with my stink guns!" Then she turned her head right toward me. Even though her face was covered, I could feel her glaring at me. "By the way, *Elmo*, thanks for the gas mask. Without it, I wouldn't have been able to pull this wonderful little peripeteia."

I couldn't help saying "What?"

"PERIPETEIA!" she screamed. "A sudden or unexpected reversal of circumstances! And that, my friend, is what this is. Zelda Snidely has snatched victory from the jaws of defeat! Give my regards to Principal Marsh—and tell him his school stinks!" She let out a long cackle and started backing quickly down the hall and away from us.

I didn't want to move, but I didn't want to let her get away. "What do we do, Oscar?" I whispered.

"Just wait for me. I've got it covered." He reached into his coat and pulled out that pocket calculator thing he used to open the secret door. He started pressing buttons furiously.

Suddenly, I heard a weird mechanical whirrr coming from the ceiling. Fernando nudged me and pointed upward. "Check *this* out," he said in amazement.

I couldn't believe it. I saw glass walls coming down out of the ceiling. One was between us and Ms. Snidely, and the other was further down the hall. Right now, Ms. Snidely was right between them.

"What's *that?*" I asked Oscar.

"I've rigged up an airtight containment system in the factory," Oscar explained quickly. "We use it to seal off any gases that escape. I think I can use it to trap Zelda!"

"Cool," I said. We *definitely* had to get some of this stuff for the KC Express.

"But look!" Keisha said. "Those walls are never going to close off in time!" She was right. Ms. Snidely could easily clear the far wall before it came all the way down. "We've got to stop her!"

"Leave that to me!" said PJ. She took off her backpack whipped it down the hall like a bowling ball. Unfortunately, it didn't knock down Ms. Snidely. Instead, it came to a slow stop right at her feet.

Ms. Snidely was so startled that she turned around and laughed at us. "Nice try, kiddies!" she cackled. "Better work on that throwing arm!" Meanwhile, the glass walls were still going down *way* too slowly. How humiliating. She even had time to make fun of us before she escaped.

Suddenly, PJ yelled something surprising back to her. "Jump, Zorro, jump! Get Ms. Snidely!"

Ms. Snidely looked startled. She looked down at the backpack just in time to see it burst open. An instant later, she was knocked flat on her back by Zorro, who leaped out of the backpack with puppy-like enthusiasm. The little robot started jumping all over her head. It was pretty hilarious, to tell you the truth.

"Back, dog! Back! Get this crazy mutt off me!" Ms. Snidely yelled. (I think I saw a piece of ticker tape fall out of Zorro's mouth. We all know what *that* said.) The ex-principal batted frantically at Zorro, but she couldn't keep our robotic friend down. Zorro kept jumping right back up, keeping Ms. Snidely occupied while the glass walls came ever closer to the floor.

Finally, in one last desperate attempt, Ms. Snidely pointed her gas guns at Zorro and let out a megadose of B.O. spray. It knocked Zorro across the hall and against one of the glass walls, just as it touched the floor. Ms.

Snidely ran up to the wall near us, but it was too late. She was sealed in—along with Zorro *and* the B.O. gas. We ran up to check it out.

Zorro seemed fine. Since she's a robot, bad smells don't bother her, of course. The knock against the wall hadn't hurt her a bit, and she was jumping on her little tank-tread feet, excited as can be.

"Good Zorro!" PJ yelled through the glass. Zorro responded with a playful digitized bark. I knew better than to say it out loud, but she looked happy as a pup.

Ms. Snidely, on the other hand, didn't look so good. She was stumbling around, waving her hand in front of her face, trying desperately to adjust her gas mask. It didn't look like it was working. Through the glass I could hear her mumbling: "Losing . . . lucidity . . . nocuous gases . . . getting . . . stronger . . . can't . . . use . . . big . . . words . . . *ugh*." With that, she slumped to the ground.

"Whoa. Glad *we* didn't end up relying on those gas masks of yours," Fernando said.

"Yeah, I guess they didn't work as well as they should have," I said. I was pretty embarrassed about it, even though it worked to our advantage.

"Is Ms. Snidely going to be okay?" Keisha asked.

"She'll be fine," Oscar said. "The B.O. gas isn't poisonous. I think she just bit off more than she could smell, as you Americans might say." He chuckled. "I'm sure the police will help her revive."

"Well, I guess this case is closed," Fernando said. "Looks like you'll need a new Teen Fresh foreman, Mr. de la Scenta."

"Yes, I do," Oscar said. "Hopefully, I'll find someone who's trustworthy. And not obsessed with euphuism."

It was PJ's turn. "You-phew-what?"

Oscar laughed. "Euphuism. It's a fancy word for using fancy words."

If Ms. Snidely were conscious, I'll bet she might have even been proud.

CHAPTER FIFTEEN

All's Well that Ends Smell

By the time ex-Principal Snidely came to, the police had come to arrest her for corporate sabotage. She went pretty quietly, all things considered. Maybe the smell was still making her a little woozy. Although as they were taking her away, I think I overheard her correcting an officer's grammar. Old habits die hard, I guess.

With the smell gone, Peak Valley's Homecoming went off without a hitch. Sure, some of the teams were a little rusty, what with all the practice they missed. But they still beat Snurdburg in basketball and debate, and according to Keisha, Brian's band rocked the house at the dance. Who knows—maybe someday Bucket will become a household word. (Although I guess it already is . . .)

The next Monday, Oscar de la Scenta showed up at Peak Valley with a new deodorant: Teen Magic. It was really the same as Teen Fresh (the pre-stinky kind), but he figured the Teen Fresh name wasn't usable anymore. Last we heard from Oscar, "Teen Magic" was a hit, and so far, it smelled only like vanilla.

As for Brian, I didn't hear from him for a week or so. Then, one afternoon, I was in the Shop Car trying to fix the gas masks (who knows when we'll need them again?) when the KC Hotline rang. I picked up the extension and heard Brian on the other end . . .

"Curtis! Buddy! What's shakin'?" he said.

I couldn't believe my ears. "What's *shakin'*? Don't you mean 'what's green'?"

"Are you kidding? That is so last week. I told you, Curtis, you've got to keep up with the times."

"But 'what's shakin'? Isn't that from the Seventies?" I asked.

"You got it. And Seventies retro is where it's at," he said. "I've even got a groovy lava lamp on order. Leslie gave me a catalog."

"Well, I guess I'd better tell Fernando," I said. "He's been using all those weird expressions of yours ever since we closed the case. I wouldn't want him to get left behind."

"Far out, man," Brian said. "And hey, I just wanted to thank you for getting rid of that smell."

"Well, it took you long enough," I said. "Where've you been? Out playing on rooftops with Bucket?"

"I wish," Brian replied. "I've been working in the cafeteria. Right after you left, the kitchen crew caught us with all that dumpster sludge. They made us clean the whole place from top to bottom. It took all of us the whole week, every day after school."

I had to laugh. "Well, at least you didn't have Ms. Snidely supervising," I said.

"Speaking of which, have you heard anything about her?"

"Oh yeah. She made some sort of deal with the police. Now she's doing community service to make up for the whole Teen Fresh thing."

"Well, I guess that's good," I said. "What's she doing?"

"She's working at a day care center," Brian said. "In fact, I went by her house last week. I saw a bunch of three-year-old kids fixing up her car."

For a second I believed him. Then he started laughing hysterically. I laughed too. It felt good. After all, if there's one thing I've learned on the Super Crew, it's that you always need your sense of humor. Even when everything else stinks.

Home Crew Hands-On

Hey, Home Crew!

Remember when Keisha made the garlic-flavored hot chocolate in the Control Car? I'll never forget it. That was one of the most disgusting things I've ever tasted.

Actually, I should say it was one of the most disgusting things I've ever <u>smelled</u>. See, I was asking ALEC why Keisha couldn't taste the garlic in her hot chocolate while she had a stuffy nose. And he said it's because most "tastes" are really smells that waft up through the back of your nose when you chew your food. Your tongue can only taste four basic flavors: sweet, salty, sour, and bitter. Everything else comes from the smell.

Hard to believe? I thought so. That's

why I decided to test it out on PJ. I went to the kitchen car and cut up an apple, a potato, and an onion into little bite-sized pieces. Then I hid the onion pieces behind the toaster and called PJ in . . .

"What's up, Curtis?" she said as she walked through the doors.

"I want you to try a little experiment for me," I said. "I'll bet you can't tell the difference between an apple and a potato. I'll stake a week's worth of kitchen-cleaning duty on it."

PJ looked a little confused. "Sounds like a no-brainer," she said. "What's the catch?" She knew me too well to think I'd give her a sucker bet.

"Just two conditions. I want you to hold your nose and close your eyes," I replied.

Now she really looked suspicious. "What for? Are you going to feed me something nasty?"

"No, don't worry about it," I said, trying to keep a straight face. "I'm just testing out something ALEC told me. He says most tastes are really smells, so you won't be able to tell the difference without your nose."

"Well, that's weird," PJ said. "I mean, sure, food doesn't taste as good when you have a cold, but I'll bet I can tell an apple from a potato. You're on. And you're going to be cleaning up after me for a whole week."

"Okay, then, close your eyes, hold your nose, and let's try it," I said.

PJ closed her eyes tight, pinched her nose shut, and stuck out her tongue. "I'm not going to put it right in your mouth!" I said. PJ actually looked a little relieved. She held out her other hand and I put the piece of apple in it. She popped it in her mouth and then chewed on it slowly.

"Keep your nose closed tight!" I told her.

"I know, I know," she said. Then she swallowed the apple chunk and paused for a second. "I think that was the potato," she said. "But give me the other one just so I can make sure."

Instead of giving her the potato, I reached behind the toaster and handed her the onion piece. She chewed on it for a while. It looked like she was concentrating really hard.

"Yep, I think this one's the apple," she finally said, with her mouth still full. "But there's a weird sort of tingle to it."

"Okay!" I said triumphantly. "Now take your hand off your nose and keep chewing!"

PJ unpinched her nose, and a second later, she had the most grossed-out look I'd seen on her face since Keisha made her garlic chocolate. "Yuck!" she said. "What *is* this?"

"It's an onion," I said. "And now you've got onion breath!"

"Ewww!" PJ said. She spit out the onion in the trash.

"Not only that," I said, "but you lost the bet and now you've got to clean the kitchen for an extra week!"

"No way!" PJ said. "You cheated! The whole thing's off!" She grabbed the potato pieces off the counter and hurled them at me.

"You're just making more of a mess to clean up!" I teased.

That just got her angrier. I won't go into the food fight that started after that, but let's just say we both ended up cleaning the kitchen that night.

You can try this experiment at home. Cut up an apple, a potato, and an onion. Then have a friend close their eyes, hold their nose tight, and taste each one. You can try it on your own, too. Just make sure you don't peek!

Could you taste the difference without your nose? Try it with other foods with the same sort of texture. Different flavors of jellybeans work great. Or different kinds of jelly or jam. You can even try it with liquids—for example, different kinds of soda pop or fruit juice.

Let us know how your taste experiment turned out. Were there any foods that you could tell apart even with your nose closed? Why do you think you could? You can reach us at our Web site: www.kineticcity.com. Or, you can call us on the phone at 1-800-877-CREW. That's 1-800-877-2739. If you leave us a message, you might be able to hear yourself on a future Kinetic City Super Crew radio show!

Good luck!

Your friend,

Curtis

Puzzle Pages

What's the Word?

If you remember the funky slang that Brian Kim used, and Ms. Snidely's use of big vocab words, you won't have any trouble with this puzzle!

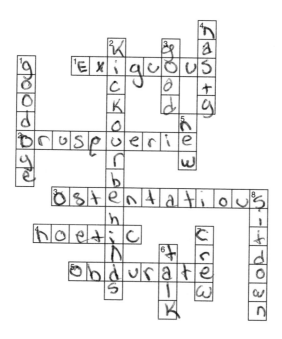

Across (Ms. Snidely's vocab)

1. Skimpy. *See page 51*
2. Abruptness of manner. *See page 53*
3. Showy, an eyesore. *See page 52*
4. Intellectual, brainy. *See page 172*
5. Stubbornly persistent in wrongdoing. *See page 176*

Down (Brian's slang)

1. Click. *See page 57*
2. House us. *See page 81*
3. Worst. *See page 36*
4. Sweet. *See page 35*
5. Green. *See pages 55-56*
6. Drop jaw. *See page 37*
7. Posse. *See page 36*
8. Leave it somewhere. *See page 75*

Food Descriptions

Have you ever read a restaurant review? Some words like buttery and nutty are used to describe taste. Try describing food yourself to see how tough it is. Come up with a couple of words to describe the smell, taste, and texture of the following foods. Don't use the word itself to describe it!

	Taste	Smell	Texture
Oranges	_____	_____	_____
Coffee	_____	_____	_____
Garlic	_____	_____	_____
Pizza	_____	_____	_____
Potato Chips	_____	_____	_____
Milk	_____	_____	_____
Chocolate	_____	_____	_____

Word Sniff

Sniff out the words below

Chemotaxis
Gas leak
Gas mask
Mass spectrometer
Mercaptans
Oil refinery

Olfactory system
Rotten eggs
Smells
Stink
Sulfur compounds
Zorro

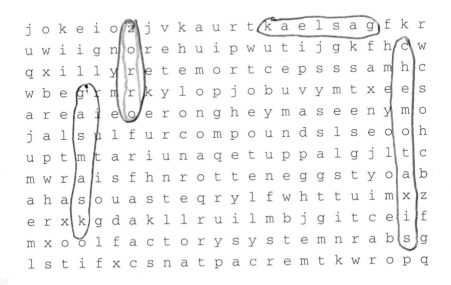

```
j o k e i o z j v k a u r t k a e l s a g f k r
u w i i g n o r e h u i p w u t i j g k f h c w
q x i l l y r e t e m o r t c e p s s a m h c
w b e g r m r k y l o p j o b u v y m t x e e s
a r e a i e o e r o n g h e y m a s e e n y m o
j a l s u l f u r c o m p o u n d s l s e o o h
u p t m a r i u n a q e t u p p a l g j l t c
m w r a i s f h n r o t t e n e g g s t y o a b
a h a s o u a s t e q r y l f w h t t u i m x z
e r x k g d a k l l r u i l m b j g i t c e i f
m x o o l f a c t o r y s y s t e m n r a b s g
l s t i f x c s n a t p a c r e m t k w r o p q
```

Answers on page 204.

Odor-ology

Make your own perfume or cologne. All you need is a jar with a cover, rubbing alcohol, and some thing that you like the scent of like flower petals, cloves, ginger root, or orange peel. Or experiment with other things that have a good smell. Try combinations of ingredients, too. The oils from these things will mix in with the alcohol. When you put the mixture on your skin, the alcohol evaporates and leaves the oil, and the scent, on your skin.

EAU DE MOI

Super Crew
instant ideas
just add brain power and stir

A Nose Knows

Animals depend on their noses to find their way around and to recognize each other. Smell is also the sense most linked to memories. Do you know people that you could recognize by just their cologne? How often do you smell something that reminds you of something else? Keep track of smells for a day. Write down every smell, describe it and what or who it makes you think of.

Puzzle Answers

What's the Word?

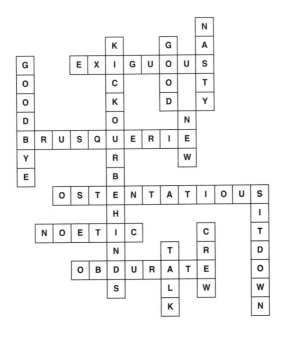

Word Sniff

```
j o k e i o z j v k a u r t k a e l s a g f k r
u w i i g n o r e h u i p w u t i j g k f h c w
q x i l l y r e t e m o r t c e p s s a m h c
w b e g r m r k y l o p j o b u v y m t x e e s
a r e a i e o e r o n g h e y m a s e e n y m o
j a l s u l f u r c o m p o u n d s l s e o o h
u p t m t a r i u n a q e t u p p a l g j l t c
m w r a i s f h n r o t t e n e g g s t y o a b
a h a s o u a s t e q r y l f w h t t u i m x z
e r x k g d a k l l r u i l m b j g i t c e i f
m x o o l f a c t o r y s y s t e m n r a b s g
l s t i f x c s n a t p a c r e m t k w r o p q
```

Other Case Files

From Rock the House:
The Case of the Meteorite Menace

"Whoa!" Megan yelled. "We've been hit!"

Bang! Another one.

"What is going on!?" Megan yelled again. "It's like those meteorites are aiming for us!"

It was bizarre all right, but I wasn't worried about getting hurt. The X-100's roof has triple-reinforced titanium plates. There was no way those falling rocks could get to us. At least until Max leaped to our rescue.

"I'll activate the force field!" he screamed out, lurching for the Control Panel.

"Max!" I yelled, trying to stop him. "We don't even have a force field." Too late. He flipped one of the switches closest to ALEC's keyboard. The result was immediate. A big section of the ceiling slid open. The train's P.A. system came on to announce what was up.

"Activating sun roof now," it said in its cold, robotic voice. "Enjoy the sunshine!"

"Uh oh," Max said.

"Close it, Max!" Megan screamed. "Now!"

Too late. The thing we all most feared finally happened.

There was an ear-splitting bang as a meteorite fell into the Control Car! The rock had caught the side of the control panel, missing Max by less than four feet. Max was fine, but the impact had activated one of the control panel switches.

"Activating thruster rockets now," the train's voice announced.

WWWHHHOOOSSSHHH!!!

The rockets fired. The sudden acceleration knocked all four of us back against the Control Car door. I don't know if you've ever seen a drag race, but the KC Express Train would've left any dragster choking in our dust. Cold, wet air blew in our faces as we tore down the side of the hill like some kind of wild roller coaster ride of no return.

⸺◈⸺

From Hot-Tempered Farmers:
The Case of the Barbecued Barns

"Hey Megan," Derek said as they tromped across twigs and leaves and a few fallen apples, "are you sure this is the right way? It seems like we've been walking for half an hour."

"Hold on, Derek," she said, squatting down and breaking into an excited whisper. "We've found it. Look over there!"

Derek crouched down beside Megan and peered in the direction she pointed. Through the last few rows of trees, they could see a young man with a ponytail and a tie-dyed tee shirt. He was squatting down beside an old barn. From Mrs. McDog's brief description, they knew it had to be the Apple Barn. It was big and red and had a huge front door shaped like an apple. About a hundred yards off to the right, just like Mrs. McDog had said, they could also make out the pile of ashes that used to be the family's Ultra Comfort Suite.

"What's he doing?" Megan whispered.

"I'm not sure," Derek replied. "It looks like he's trying to drill a stick into that board."

Megan furrowed her eyebrows in that way she does when she's confused.

"Is that some kind of dairy farmer thing?" she asked.

Derek shrugged his shoulders. "Don't ask me. I'm from the city. I get milk from the supermarket."

Megan was about to say something else, but was cut off when the young man started to shout excitedly.

"All right! Finally!"

Megan and Derek watched wide-eyed as he put his stick down and began to fan a small flame with his hands!

"Derek!" Megan whispered as loud as she dared. "It really is an arsonist! Just look at him! He's come back to torch another barn!"

"Fire!" the young man cried out as the flames began to grow. "Yeeeee-Hah!"

"He's setting the Apple Barn on fire!" Megan continued. "We've got to stop him!"

———◆———

GET REAL!!!

This and every adventure of the Kinetic City Super Crew is based on real science.

Mercaptans are used all the time in natural gas (the kind that's used for heating and ovens in some houses), which is naturally odorless. Humans are extremely sensitive to mercaptans, which, as ALEC says in Chapter One, makes them a really good warning system.

The microcapsules used in Teen Fresh are used in many kinds of deodorants today. They also have all kinds of other uses. For example, some pre-packaged cake mixes that you can buy in the supermarket include baking soda in microcapsules. Because the microcapsules won't melt until the mixture reaches a certain temperature, that lets you "add" the baking soda while the cake is already baking. This may help the cake rise in just the right way, and turn out lighter. Microcapsules are also used in some medicines to allow them to get into your bloodstream gradually instead of all at once.

The artificial noses ALEC talks about in Chapter Seven are still being worked on by scientists at Tufts University and elsewhere. Eventually, they hope to use these "virtual noses" to sniff out dangerous chemicals in food, water, and in the air. And someday, the computer noses may even help doctors tell when you're sick, since many diseases change the chemistry of your breath and sweat.

And yes, there really are scientists who study body odor, just like the ones at Oscar de la Scenta's factory. One place where you can find them is at the Monell Chemical Senses Center in Philadelphia, Pennsylvania, where they conduct all kinds of research on smells and smelling. Some scientists there are doing the same kind of research Frank the foreman talked about, including trying to find other foods—besides sweat—for your body bacteria to munch on.

NOW HEAR THIS!!

Every week tune in to the Kinetic City Super Crew radio show!

If you think reading about the Crew is cool, wait till you hear them blasting out of your radio. Every week the Super Crew find themselves tangled up in danger and mystery in a different place... from the icy tundras of Alaska to the busy streets of Kinetic City.

Call 1-800-877-CREW (2739)

to find out where you can tune in to hear the next awesome episode of Kinetic City Super Crew.

KCSC is featured on Aahs World Radio and finer public radio stations around the country.

 AMERICAN ASSOCIATION FOR THE ADVANCEMENT OF SCIENCE   National Science Foundation

Check out
Kinetic City Cyber Club
a science mystery game
on the World Wide Web

Come and Play!
http://www.kineticcity.com

How would you like to try solving your own mystery with the Super Crew? It's waitng for you now, at Kineticcity.com!

You'll also find games, info on your favorite Super Crew members, online chats, and cool things to download, like stationery and screen savers. There's even a page for teachers and parents.

When you get to the site make sure you bookmark it. You'll want to go there every day because there's always something new and fun happening at Kinetic City Cyber Club!

AMERICAN ASSOCIATION FOR THE
ADVANCEMENT OF SCIENCE

National Science Foundation

The staff of the Kinetic City Super Crew Radio Project:

Executive Producer:	Bob Hirshon
Senior Producer:	Joe Shepherd
Producer/Engineer:	Barnaby Bristol
Assistant Producer:	Anna Ewald
Director:	Susan Keady
Writers:	Chuck Harwood
	Marianne Meyer
	Sara St. Antoine
	Justin Warner
Associate Editor:	Samantha Beres
The Crew:	Damion Connor
	Elana Eisen-Markowitz
	Joaquin Foster-Gross
	Reggie Harris
	Melody Johnson
	Monique McClung
	Jennifer Roberts
	Paul Simon
Business Manager:	Thu Vu
Outreach Coordinator:	Corette Jones
Project Assistant:	Renee Stockdale-Homick
Cyber Club Producer:	Kimberly Amaral
EHR, Head:	Shirley Malcom
Director, Public Understanding of Science:	Alan McGowan
Science Content Advisor:	David Lindley
Executive Officer, AAAS:	Richard Nicholson